THE BIRTH OF COGENANT

LEX PUSHKA

Cover design and book layout by Lex Pushka
First Edition: March 2024
ISBN: 979-8-27578-304-9

www.lexpushka.com

To Tahsin, my best friend and my family.

Your friendship and unwavering support bring constant joy and strength to my life. This book wouldn't have been possible without you by my side through every challenge and success. This dedication is a small token of my deep love and gratitude.

CHAPTER 1

'It's not like we have many options left,' Hiro said through clenched teeth. He leaned against the wall and immediately regretted it when he felt the cold mould-slime squish under his shoulder with a slurp. He fought the urge to recoil, forcing himself to stay pressed against the slime. It made his skin crawl, but he refused to show Diego any sign of discomfort. He maintained a defiant, sarcastic stare and said, 'Feel free to walk out there. But don't blame me when that droid zaps the living hell out of you.'

The mouldy smell filled Diego's nostrils, fuelling his rising irritation. 'That's exactly what you're asking me to do, you bastard,' he replied without missing a beat.

Hiro rolled his eyes. 'No, I'm asking you to create a distraction.'

Diego's lips curled into a smirk. 'Why do I have to be the bait again? We could use the—'

'Stop it!' Hiro interrupted mid-sentence. 'Can't you see? We're cornered. You can be melodramatic all you want if we get out of this mess. But for now, please focus.'

The dim, grimy light seeping through the battered windows of the abandoned skyscraper barely illuminated Diego's face. But Hiro didn't need light. He knew his friend's expression was tight and his jaw muscles were clenched with anger—a sure sign he was furious.

Hiro had been bottling up his simmering frustration with their less-than-ideal situation. They were trapped on the 76th floor of a crumbling building. Every so often, he caught himself wrinkling his nose. The thick, stale stench of rot and rust clawed at his throat like a physical manifestation of their awful circumstances. He had already considered all their escape options, even leaping out of a window. A fall from this height was a guaranteed one-way ticket to the afterlife, but to Hiro, it seemed only slightly worse than getting zapped by the Eyeball.

CerebroNet had installed zappers in its countless hover droids, nicknamed Eyeballs for their spherical shape and the technical designation EYE2-C. The zapper, a notorious energy weapon, was reputed to be an instrument of torture. Designed as a deterrent, it inflicted agonising pain without killing its targets.

Even a random mention of zapping sent shivers running down people's spines. Everyone had seen its victims contorted in agony as a zap surged through them with a burst of bright, crackling energy. Their tormented bodies clenched and unclenched in persistent seizures. Their skin morphed into a ghastly, shifting marble pattern caused by the veins snaking underneath it. Their eyes rotated upwards into their heads, and their tongues stuck out. Once the convulsing subsided, the victims found themselves suspended between life and death. Their hands and legs curled in unnatural positions, enduring shredded muscles, torn ligaments, and ruptured tendons. The recovery process was a long, arduous journey, both physically and mentally.

Diego knew full well that the Eyeball would easily turn his own body against him, reducing him to a grotesque monument to CerebroNet's power. So he held back his biting retorts. Panting, he hunched in the corner of the decomposing office space. Diego's silence was uncharacteristic. Usually, he would counter Hiro's provocations, but now, there were two good reasons not to. The first was spite. The second was fear.

Hiro's chest tightened with guilt as he sensed Diego's anxiety. They were like two puzzle pieces that fit perfectly, having known each other inside-out from a young age. He exhaled, breaking the monotonous hum of the Eyeball in the next room. 'I know I messed up,' Hiro said, trying to steady his voice to conceal his panic. 'And I'm sorry for dragging you into this. But right now, I need you to keep a level head and help us escape this trap. I can't do it without you. We've been in tighter spots. We'll figure a way out of this one too.'

Diego stayed silent.

They had spent countless hours hunting CerebroNet droids and dodging their retaliation. This time, however, something unsettling distinguished their present circumstances from past encounters. This particular droid was behaving weirdly, forcing Hiro's brain to sizzle like an overclocked processor. The Eyeball's intentions eluded him, leaving him feeling vulnerable.

The Eyeball, its metal-alloy body glistening in the dim light, had stopped its pursuit and was acting completely out of character. Rather than zapping them, it held its position. The machine repeatedly scanned the room, the faint hum of its instruments and the subtle odour of ozone filling the space. It seemed to be adopting a protective stance at the exit.

Never before had a CerebroNet droid hesitated to zap unaugmented humans, with or without a reason. Hiro's heart was pounding, but he didn't want Diego to know he was afraid, too. So, to lighten the tense atmosphere, he added, 'Besides, the last time I listened to you, we ended up swimming through a lake of shit.'

'It wasn't shit, asshole!' Diego snapped.

Despite their uncertain situation, Hiro's eyes twinkled with delight. He chuckled. He loved winding Diego up.

Hiro's mischievous giggle gave it away, and Diego stared at him, understanding he was being teased. 'Sometimes, I really hate you.'

Hiro's smile widened. 'Nah, you're just mad because you love me.'

Diego's fleeting grin morphed into a grimace as he turned serious again. He knew Hiro like the back of his hand, so he always became nervous when Hiro tried to hide his fear with motivational speeches or humour. When Diego was anxious, he talked. In this particular situation, an avalanche of questions barrelled through his head. In response to the teasing, he unleashed them on Hiro. 'Is it still out there? Do you think it trapped us on purpose? It knows we're here, right? Why isn't it zapping us?'

Hiro shrugged. Ignoring the torrent of questions, he tiptoed to the opening in the wall and stole a glance at the lurking machine. Despite the threat, Hiro paused to study the Eyeball. As usual, the droid's gravity-assist engine allowed it to defy the laws of physics. It exuded an air of magic as it hovered in place with an elegance that belied its ability to wreak havoc. But this Eyeball's appearance was distinct. It lacked the flashing yellow lights that normally dotted their circular form. Instead, its elliptical body gleamed with an odd, swirling blue glow that reflected off the shiny alloy surface.

As a member of the Technophobe community, Hiro knew little about digital technology. But he had to rely on his ability to predict the next move of the machines. It was important for two reasons: his survival and the ability to make a living from hunting them. Over time, he had become efficient in deciphering Eyeball behaviour.

At first, in response to the growing unrest, London's government deployed CerebroNet Corporation's hover-droids to intensify surveillance on citizens who rejected ID implants and consequently lost their right to government aid. As hunger and chaos, exacerbated by devastating weather, tore through the city, it fractured, splitting into two parts. The police force crumbled under the tidal wave of riots and raids on water filtration facilities and food production domes. It was then that upgraded Eyeballs replaced the police, becoming autonomous law enforcement agents. Thousands of them patrolled New London and Old Town, reporting directly to CerebroNet's core AI. But as the situation worsened, the next upgrade equipped each Eyeball with the distinctive blinking yellow lights and a zapper, with the authority to use the weapon on any human at its digital will.

This upgrade solidified the divide between the two parts of London. Hiro and Diego, like all Technophobe outcasts in the ruins of the forsaken Old Town, rejected government control. They refused to accept the mandatory subdermal ID implants. Instead, they relied on analogue devices to fake IDs without implanting anything. It was the highest crime but a necessary trick to avoid being zapped on sight. Hiro and Diego would often lurk close to the New London border, provoking and luring Eyeballs into their traps.

The guys had encountered a dazzling array of advanced tech in New London. They had seen cargo bots, augmented humans, intelligent transport, and more. Yet, only the Eyeballs used gravity-assist engines. CerebroNet Corporation kept its technology secret, even from the government of New London. Hiro and Diego were the rare few, if not the only ones, who could capture Eyeballs, extract the engine, and live to tell the tale. This skill marked them as quasi-celebrities among their community of Technophobes. These exiles rejected everything digital, including any surveillance or implantations. However, for them, fame was not the prize.

The Eyeballs had organic components within their gravity-assist engines that Cybergangs used to cook a potent drug called Leviathan. Named after the mythological sea monster, Leviathan wielded an astonishing effect. Upon ingestion, it manipulated the user's neurochemical composition, inducing a unique state of altered consciousness. Users reported sensations of travelling through parallel worlds. Leviathan also warped temporal perception, causing time to stretch during the euphoric high, while only a few minutes may have elapsed in reality. These intense experiences made Leviathan highly addictive and extremely sought after in New London as much as in Old Town. The Cybergangs paid a steep price for these organic parts. This compensated for the risk Hiro and Diego took and allowed them to repay Mr Fassal. In return, he provided them with spoofed IDs, water, food, and a roof over their heads.

Over countless confrontations with the Eyeballs, this was the first time Hiro had encountered one emitting the mesmerising bluish glow. As he watched the droid, their potential ways out faded further into a mere mirage. The walls seemed to inch closer, squeezing away the promise of escape. Hiro sensed the inevitability of capture tightening its hold around him. He had expected pursuit, skirmishes, and a chase across the Old Town.

But not to be trapped like a rat in a derelict skyscraper. The sense of captivity nibbled at Hiro's pride, making him clench his fists so hard that his knuckles turned white and felt close to bursting.

Hiro quivered and snapped back to the present, realising that he had lost track of time, with his thoughts drifting as if he were high on Leviathan. The experience felt like being hypnotised by a predator. The deceitful yet hypnotic glow lured him deeper into an ambush. It enchanted him and drew him into an inevitable trap.

Diego released a slow, measured sigh as he watched Hiro's exasperation escalate. He was well aware of the ugly reality of their situation. Not only did they need to escape the trap unharmed, but they also had to catch their captor. Their recent string of unsuccessful hunts had left them behind on their payments to Mr Fassal.

Finally, Diego responded, his voice heavy with sarcasm. 'All right,' he said, making air quotes, 'let's hear your "genius" plan then.'

The plan was straightforward. It relied on coordination and precise timing. Hiro intended to disrupt the gravitational field that allowed Eyeballs to hover. Success depended on sabotaging the droid. Diego would jump into the adjoining room, shooting mid-leap to anger it and draw its attention away from Hiro. After Diego had taken cover, rolling to the side behind the mound left by the fallen ceiling, Hiro would fire an EMP net, grounding the droid and confusing its sensors. This would provide Diego with a chance to short the Eyeball with a capacitor. If timed well, they could immobilise the machine. But one mistimed move could get them zapped.

'You don't need to hit the bastard. It just needs to register that it's being attacked. I'll shoot the net and send the pulse when it goes after you,' explained Hiro.

Diego contemplated the details of the proposal. His face knotted as he turned over the steps in his mind. 'What a grand plan. If I don't get zapped, I'll break my fucking neck performing these acrobatics.'

Hiro struck his forehead with his palm. 'Don't start again!'

'Who's the drama queen now?' Despite his initial objection, Diego readied himself. He assessed their surroundings and stretched his limbs in preparation for the jump. 'I can't believe I'm doing this,' he muttered, then glanced at Hiro. 'You ready?'

'Ready when you are,' Hiro replied, his finger twitching on the EMP net launcher's trigger.

Diego took a deep breath and positioned himself at the room's entrance. His heart pounded a relentless rhythm. Sweat trickled down his forehead as he checked his makeshift gun. 'On three,' he announced, stealing another glance at Hiro. He stepped back, sensing an adrenaline rush as he prepared to leap. Gathering energy from every fibre of his being, he started the countdown. 'One... Two... Three!'

Diego lunged forward. His heart pounded in his ears as he glided through the air. Then his body swivelled mid-jump. His muscles fired with determination, adjusting his trajectory by twisting in freefall with feline fluidity. Simultaneously, his sweat-slicked finger tightened on the weapon's cold trigger. The muzzle flared, spitting a vicious barrage of bullets towards the Eyeball. The gun's mechanical snarl echoed through the room, the shots bouncing off the exposed steel beams and walls. Diego saw the debris falling around him as he heard the bullets impacting the Eyeball, etching a mark of defiance on it with an echoing metallic thud.

The skyscraper's scattered remnants—fragments of glass, contorted metal, and chunks of concrete—presented a dangerous problem for Diego's landing. His hand slid on the debris as he executed the side roll. With a surprised, pained grunt, his world spiralled into chaos. His body tumbled forward, smashing headfirst into a hunk of collapsed ceiling. The sudden blow jarred his senses, and a shockwave of pain exploded through his spine as a warm, metallic taste filled his mouth. The breath was knocked out of his chest by the impact on his lungs, leaving him gasping like a fish floundering on dry land. His pulse roared in his ears, and his vision blurred as he blinked back the tears pooling in his eyes. Even in the rapidly worsening situation, Diego knew it would feel infinitely worse if the Eyeball zapped him. He wanted to push through the all-consuming pain to find cover. But at that moment, splayed on the cold floor, he could only gasp for air.

The Eyeball darted across the room. The uneven beams of setting sunlight danced off its shiny exterior, giving the impression that it was dashing through a rain of silver shards. Like a wounded beast, the droid emitted a distressed electronic cacophony of digital whistles and clicks as it manoeuvred through the mounds of debris.

The unfolding scene spiked Hiro's adrenaline. He seized the opportunity presented by the droid's focus on Diego. Despite the evolving chaos, he aimed the EMP net launcher at the erratic Eyeball. He fired. The net sprang from the launcher, spreading out like a spider's web, expanding in a cascade of thin tendrils enveloping their captor. But the machine countered just before he could activate the EMP charge.

Entangled within the net and resembling an out-of-control gyroscope, the Eyeball began a maddening spin. It yanked the EMP trigger out of Hiro's hand. Its desperate attempt to break free transformed into a blur of motion. Flakes of rust, mould, and dust swirled around it in a chaotic dance of decay.

The net broke off, and the droid froze in place. For a fleeting moment, everything seemed suspended in an ethereal stillness, as if the old skyscraper was holding its breath. The dust particles, caught by the late afternoon sunlight, began their gentle descent. Swirling in a tranquil motion, they settled around the Eyeball in a silent ballet.

A few rapid electronic clicks cut through the peaceful scene. Then an intolerable, high-pitched noise filled the room. Glass in the frail skyscraper's skeletal window frames trembled and cracked under the onslaught. The air itself seemed to disintegrate. The deafening sound wave sliced through Hiro and Diego like a scalpel through flesh. They both collapsed, clutching their ears. The barrage of pure noise hammered their eardrums, resonated in their bones, and wrapped every nerve ending in anguish.

Hiro forced himself to open his eyes. He couldn't see through the ripples in his tears caused by the vibration. He forced himself to remove his hands from his ears to wipe them away. As he focused his brown eyes, he saw Diego screaming and rolling side-to-side, covering his ears in a futile attempt to block out the assault of the Eyeball's acoustic weapon. The droid was hovering just a few steps from Diego. Hiro's mind raced. Diego's life depended on him. He needed to shut down the machine. But the Eyeball's sonic blast left him feeling like a sack of aching meat filled with vibrating bones. He could barely move, let alone devise a plan and execute it.

In a desperate, last-ditch effort, Hiro grabbed a rusted rebar from the debris. Wincing, he pushed himself up. With a primal, adrenaline-fuelled yell, he thrust the makeshift spear through the Eyeball, pinning it to the wall with the full force of his body weight.

Silence enveloped the room.

Diego didn't know how much time had passed before the ringing in his ears began to subside. When his hearing returned, he recognised Hiro's moans. He turned towards the sound and saw his friend rocking back and forth on the floor, holding his shoulder. Forcing himself to overcome the disorientation, Diego scrambled through the debris. Panic overtook him at the sight of his friend's anguished grimace. 'Hiro... Hiro,' he gasped in a hoarse voice as he examined Hiro's injuries.

The rebar's texture had baked into Hiro's charred palm. His arm and shoulder were limp from the runaway energy that had surged through the rebar as it pierced through the Eyeball.

Diego cradled Hiro's head, resting it in his lap to comfort himself as much as his friend. Hiro's face was white as bone, beaded with droplets of sweat. Diego blinked fiercely to clear the tears from his eyes and pleaded in a cracking voice, 'Please. Talk to me!'

Fighting for words, Hiro croaked, 'Got shocked through the stick when I killed the bitch.' He struggled to prop himself up. 'I don't feel my shoulder and arm.'

Diego's forehead creased with worry. 'Shit, shit, shit...' he muttered as he examined Hiro's shoulder, probing for additional wounds.

'Ouch! Stop it, asshole,' Hiro shouted, his face twisting with annoyance. 'It hurts.'

Diego's eyebrows shot up, and his eyes widened. 'So, you can feel your shoulder. That's good!'

'I'm lucky it was rusted. My head's still aching, but I think I'll be all right. How are you?'

Diego exhaled. 'Not much better than you, to be honest,' he admitted. His expression grew serious. 'What the hell was that sound? An acoustic weapon?'

Hiro's gaze bore into the neutralised Eyeball as though attempting to see through it. 'I have no idea,' he rumbled in a low growl. 'But I'm glad it's toast.'

Pinned to the wall by the rebar, the Eyeball resembled a giant lollipop. Skewered through its core, its once frightening frame oozed a fluorescent-green liquid. The thick substance slid down the droid's surface. Each droplet fell with a faint, echoing plink as it hit the floor.

'Look, the goo's leaking. I think its engine is gone. We can't sell it,' Hiro said.

Diego took a moment to appreciate the pitiful state of the once formidable enemy. 'Mr Fassal won't be happy with us again. What do we do wi—'

'Click click clickclick...' a sequence of electronic clicks interrupted Diego.

The guys froze. Fear seized them, sending a tide of goosebumps over their bodies. Their pain and discomfort faded into insignificance. Wide-eyed, they stared at the Eyeball.

The faint blue glow reappeared, forming a uniform pattern around the droid. The gravity-assist engine reactivated with a wheezing sound.

Hiro and Diego began breathing in short, shallow gasps as, with growing horror, they watched the machine come back to life.

Firmly secured to the wall, the Eyeball made a series of desperate manoeuvres. It tried to jerk up, then down, and attempted a sideways wriggle, all in a frantic bid to dislodge itself. A moment of stillness passed as the droid rethought its approach and recalculated available options. It erupted in an outburst of digital screeches, clicks, and whistles understood only by its kind. Then, in a sudden, jolting twist, the Eyeball executed a full 360-degree rotation on the impaling rebar.

Hiro immediately understood the purpose behind this frantic

manoeuvre. With each additional spin, the Eyeball moved away from the wall, inching closer to them to free itself from the rebar.

Hiro shouted, 'Run!'

* * *

The air in their living quarters was filled with the sharp tang of sweat and the scent of blood and seared skin. Hiro lay in his worn-out bed, staring into nothingness. Diego sat on the floor in a corner, face cradled in his palms with elbows resting on his knees. Both were silent. But their thoughts buzzed with memories of their narrow escape.

Though not picturesque, the habitat comforted them with the warmth of home. Their dwelling was a cramped, shadow-laden chamber tucked away within the twisting arteries of the abandoned metro network. The tight space could barely accommodate them. Their every move often looked like an intricate, pre-planned manoeuvre to prevent mishaps amid their sparse belongings. They were delighted with the small quarters and even took pride in their ability to make the most of the small space.

Hiro and Diego's friendship was more than just a bond. It was a lifeline built through the endurance of countless hardships. They faced the harsh realities of an orphanage as a team. Their shared experiences were the glue that held them together. But it was their audacious breakout that established their unbreakable connection. The escape transformed Hiro and Diego from mere friends to fighters bound by mutual dependence. In the unforgiving world outside, reliance on each other proved to be a successful survival strategy. Each victory and every averted disaster tightened the invisible cord that tethered them closer. Their shared preference for dark humour and relentless banter provided a healthy portion of fun. It became a beacon of normalcy in their outlawed existence.

In their dingy chamber, the guys grew into young men under the gruff yet protective supervision of Mr Fassal—the local Technophobe leader. His role, however, went beyond merely providing them with clean water and sustenance. Under his stern guidance, Hiro and Diego learned to adapt and thrive in the harsh world. Mr Fassal taught them the Technophobe creed. He shaped their juvenile minds into defiant resilience. He showed them how to find joy in simplicity—from weaving their own clothes to harvesting rainwater. The guys embraced a life of self-sufficiency that contrasted with the technology-saturated life outside their community.

Technophobe ideology had developed over two centuries. It stemmed from an anti-technology group known as the Silicon Sceptics. When silicon replaced germanium in chip transistors, the initial whispers of conspiracy theories grew into a full-fledged movement. Over the decades, these theories coalesced into a doctrine underpinned by neo-Luddite philosophy and anti-AI sentiment. Their strict reliance on only analogue technology earned them the title of Technophobes.

Climate catastrophe battered the world. It plunged people

into a desperate struggle for clean water, food, and shelter. Governments leveraged digital ID implants to control distribution channels. This heavy-handed move ignited robust opposition from Technophobe leaders. They warned of the ethical dangers of such a rights-stripping system. What began as protest swelled into a tidal wave of public outrage.

As things worsened by the day, more people embraced Technophobism. The philosophy reached a fever pitch of popularity when New London turned to CerebroNet Corporation's army of weaponised security robots. Practically overnight, Technophobism united most of the population under a single doctrine, often serving as a spiritual anchor.

In Hiro and Diego's community, people rejected holograms, smart homes, AIs, and any robotics. Folks used rotary phones, typewriters, vinyl records, and old cathode ray tube televisions. The digital world held no allure. Technophobes perceived it as an enslaving, corrupting force, and a tool for manipulation. The tangible authenticity of analogue technology made it secure and reliable. Despite the resurgence of curable diseases due to a lack of medical equipment, Technophobes remained resolute. They cherished the tactile world, sustaining themselves on rodents, maggots, and fungal protein, unwavering in their commitment to their traditional way of life.

Hiro's disdain for digital technology stemmed from Technophobe teachings, but his childhood experiences were the reason for his seething hatred of CerebroNet. He grew up fighting the constant cruelty of other orphans. The insults revolved around the story of Hiro, drenched in his mother's blood, being pulled from the machine's embrace. They called him Bot Baby because the machine didn't want to release him until its deactivation. Rumours spread about his mother's tragic death. She had worked for CerebroNet Corporation and was reportedly killed by a malfunctioning robot. The gruesome images and the relentless abuse etched themselves deep into Hiro's consciousness.

Diego watched Hiro with concern. He understood all too well that today's confrontation with CerebroNet's droid had resurrected distant memories. Hiro's anguished expression revealed intense emotional turmoil rather than physical pain from the injuries he'd endured from the encounter.

Diego retrieved some fresh rags and a bowl. He filled it with clean water. 'Let me have a look,' he offered.

Fighting the pain, Hiro took off his jacket and stretched his hand towards Diego. 'Thank you.'

Diego crouched before him. His brow furrowed with concern as he removed dirt, burned skin, and congealed blood from Hiro's palm. 'What a fucked-up day. That droid scared the shit out of me.'

'Yeah, judging by your smell, it did,' Hiro said, prompting laughter from both of them.

'You stink like shit, too, bro,' Diego replied with a grin.

'I can imagine. I also feel like shit,' Hiro said, wincing.

With a knock on the door, Diego's giggles faded away.

Hiro suppressed a growl and called out, 'Come in!'

Mr Fassal squeezed his hulking frame into the small room, dominating the space with his commanding presence. Bushy, stern brows locked in a rigid furrow emphasised his silent authority. His deeply nested eyes projected seasoned wisdom and unwavering confidence. Wrinkles crisscrossed his face like an intricate road map—a mark of relentless perseverance through hardship and grit.

Mr Fassal's piercing stare softened with flickers of concern when he looked upon the dirty faces and weary expressions of the two guys before him. 'Evening, gents,' he said, his voice filling the room like thunder. 'You look rough.'

Hiro flicked a glance towards Diego, then dropped his gaze. 'CerebroNet has a new model,' he muttered with resignation.

An uncomfortable silence followed Hiro's admission as Mr Fassal's expression turned sour. The lines around his eyes deepened into canyons of disapproval. His annoyance was evident in his voice when he asked, 'Now what?'

Hiro inhaled. He steadied his vocal cords and explained. 'The new model has an acoustic crowd control weapon and seems to have also learned how to deal with our EMP nets.'

Mr Fassal said nothing, but his expression hardened, and he raised an eyebrow.

Hiro hesitated for a moment before continuing, 'It's a major setback for us.'

Mr Fassal's shoulders slumped as he let out a deep, troubled sigh. He appeared to withdraw into himself. 'When will this end?' he murmured, more to himself. With a slight shake of his head, Mr Fassal returned to reality. He moved Diego's filthy jacket aside and sat on the narrow bench. 'Anyhow, back to business.'

Hiro and Diego grimaced, knowing what was coming.

'We agreed that you would pay your rent today. Haven't we?'

Diego and Hiro felt embarrassed. The routine had become too familiar.

Hiro hesitated, working up the courage to ask the question he had asked too often in the past months. 'Can we please get an extension?' he said, seeming more desperate than he intended.

Diego chimed in, also sounding desperate. 'These new upgrades took us by surprise,' he said, his words tumbling out in a rush. 'CerebroNet played a real trick on us. It chased us into a trap.'

Mr Fassal's gaze lingered on Diego's tan skin, smeared with layers of dirt and blood, and his expression softened for a moment. His eyes flicked between the two young men. He recognised the worry and hope in their eyes, but he had responsibilities. His position as the leader wasn't just a title. It was a job that entailed making hard decisions. So, despite the flicker of sympathy in his face, his resolve remained as steely as ever. 'I sympathise, but you are three months behind. Thousands of folk are counting on me. Most have valid excuses for why they shouldn't pay.' His words were harsh, but his tone was regretful. 'I've already given you special treatment. You have your way with the Eyeballs, which is very good for our people. But if you have nothing to show for your...' he paused, searching for the right word, 'celebrity status, I will have riots to deal with.'

Mr Fassal was dead serious. Their world was miserable, turning their community into a powder keg ready to ignite at the slightest perceived injustice. The difficulty of creating fake IDs using analogue technology exacerbated the situation. Its high cost rendered freedom of movement a luxury few could afford.

Diego attempted to inject some buoyancy into the grim atmosphere. 'Thank you for being a wonderful and fair leader. We are all very grateful to you. We know the enormous amount of hard work you invest to ensure our well-being and protection.' Diego inhaled and continued his plea. 'Would it be possible to give us just a few more days? We need to recover and heal a bit. We'll come up with a new strategy.'

A grin split Mr Fassal's features as he leaned back with an air of self-satisfaction. 'Ahh, flattery,' he said, amusement lacing his words. 'Never fails, does it?' His gaze flitted between Hiro and Diego. He enjoyed the unease his response had provoked as he dismantled Diego's feeble attempt at manipulation.

Diego's face flushed a vivid red, and his lips formed a perfect 'O' of surprise as he grappled for a response. The words knotted themselves on his tongue, struggling to find their way out.

With a sigh, Mr Fassal decided on a compromise. 'All right, I'll give you two more weeks to settle your debt. But there's a catch.'

Suspicion flared in Hiro's eyes. 'And what would it be?'

Mr Fassal leaned forward, his eyes locking on Hiro's. 'Help

me out with a… small task. Consider it an opportunity to aid the entire Technophobe family.'

Hiro and Diego exchanged a curious glance.

'How can we help you, Mr Fassal?' Diego asked.

Mr Fassal grinned. 'Tomorrow, we'll host a very influential guest interested in discussing a potential alliance. Our visitor is looking for intelligent and capable people, and you two fit the bill. All I ask of you is to be charming hosts and represent our community, positioning us as a strong and reliable ally.'

Diego smiled. 'We can do that!'

Hiro's curiosity piqued. 'And who is our influential visitor?'

'Ms Mordwell,' replied Mr Fassal.

Hiro's eyes widened, and his mouth opened in disbelief.

'The Mordwell? The bitch-queen of the augments?' Diego spluttered, earning a sharp glance from Mr Fassal.

Mr Fassal pursed his lips. 'Must you talk like this?'

'She is the leading voice for bionic humanity. How can she be our ally?' protested Hiro.

Mr Fassal's tone held a firmness matching the unwavering gaze with which he met Hiro's stare. 'She adamantly opposes CerebroNet. And if we can convince her we are worth funding, we will gain a powerful partner in our fight against it.'

Hiro nodded, considering Mr Fassal's words. He made his decision, tugged his boots off, climbed under the blanket, and announced matter-of-factly, 'I am not going to meet that bitch.'

The bench scraped against the floor as Mr Fassal rose to his feet. With precise and deliberate movements that projected a calculated grace, he folded his arms across his chest. His face contorted into a scowl. He glared down at Hiro with a cold, hard stare and spoke in a low voice, enunciating each word with unmistakable clarity, 'Well. Then you are both packing and leaving tonight.'

CHAPTER 2

Ms Mordwell stepped onto the Technophobes' turf, acutely aware that she was venturing into enemy territory. Here, her ideals and principles were not only unappreciated but violently opposed. She saw herself as a queen navigating the chequered board of this nauseating, infernal wasteland to secure a checkmate. Every step she took and every word she uttered was premeditated, woven into layers of strategy.

The first thing she noticed was the air. A suffocating blend of decay and festering humanity clung to the back of her throat. It contrasted starkly with the nearly sterile environment of her New London palace. The surroundings were equally grim. What was once beautiful was now ruined by the climate and decades neglect. The buildings towering around her showed no signs of their former luxury. These bare structures stared at her, their hollow windows like empty eye sockets.

Graffiti marked the territory. Ms Mordwell's vision flashed as the algorithms of her implants recognised the crudely painted symbols. The most prominent was a fist gripping a broken microchip—a trophy of defiance. A clear-cut message stood out beneath it: Freedom in Flesh, Not in Chips. The atmosphere of this place made goosebumps creep across even the sections of her synthskin.

A large group of people emerged from the remnants of an old underground station. Ms Mordwell's expression remained composed. She stood tall and imposing despite the knot of tension forming in her stomach. Mr Fassal, leading the group, approached Ms Mordwell and took a moment to scrutinise her.

Ms Mordwell's appearance was nothing short of stunning. She emanated glamour. Her obsidian hair was elegantly swept up into a voluminous hairdo, contrasting with her sparkling, sequin-embellished white evening dress. The gown hugged her silhouette, a daring thigh-high split showing off her figure. Her off-the-shoulder, sweetheart neckline highlighted her bionic shoulders, which blended seamlessly into her human body. Matching white fragments of synthskin adorned her bionic arms, mirroring the dress in a fusion of aesthetics and functionality. Her arms, with their exposed titanium alloy bones, sparkled like precious jewels in the smog-filtered sunlight, making a fashion statement in their own right.

Mr Fassal greeted her, his broad smile barely concealing his anticipation. This meeting bore the promise of significant gains— increased funding, an influx of food supplies, and a lifeline from the brink of despair. Despite Ms Mordwell's unwavering advocacy for augmented humanity, she and her followers had a common cause with the Technophobes. They vehemently opposed the merciless artificial superintelligence that ruled both parts of the city.

Mr Fassal intended to capitalise on this potential alliance. He had tirelessly conditioned his followers to overlook Ms Mordwell's stance on digital technology. He focused their attention instead on the invaluable resources she could offer. As greetings were exchanged, the atmosphere remained cordial. Even Mr Fassal's network of informants—a band of hostile teenage girls known for their unsolicited venomous remarks and avid interest in others' affairs—appeared to have curbed their usual antagonism and dramatic posturing. Provoking one of these girls was like poking a hornet's nest. The entire swarm would descend on you in a flurry of relentless obnoxiousness. But today, even these notorious community members kept in line, causing Mr Fassal to enjoy a wave of satisfaction at the smooth progression of events.

Brimming with eagerness, Mr Fassal led Ms Mordwell on a tour of his underground community. Life hummed on amidst the glow of analogue devices and the vibrant green moss clinging to the damp walls in the labyrinth of the once-bustling metro network. Ms Mordwell strolled beside him, her eyes wide, absorbing the retro-tech panorama. Their journey took them past a collage of characters, each with a distinct air of pride. Mr Fassal described their unique accomplishments, presenting them as shining examples of the community's talent and resilience.

There was Marta, who breathed life into abandoned scrap; Samuel, who spun tales from a bygone era that fed their spirits; Clara, who had once turned the tide of a cholera outbreak with nothing but wits and willpower; Eddie, who illuminated young minds in the dimly lit depths of the underground; and Tom the Tinkerer, who transformed waste into wind power.

Ms Mordwell fired off a barrage of questions about the makeshift machinery and the dependable citizens she encountered. Her role was to play the fascinated ally, the collaborator. But beneath the constructed persona, she remained detached and disinterested. Everything irked her. She fought to ignore it, but the surroundings wouldn't let her. This place didn't just demand her attention. It assaulted her. The grime. A greasy film she could almost feel on her skin. The noise. A sharp, metallic shriek that pierced her thoughts. The smell... God, the smell. A sour, thick stench that crawled up her nose and coated her tongue.

They stepped into a spacious makeshift room. It mirrored the poverty and decay of Old Town. The air was thick with the smell of corrosion. Everything, from the furniture to the light fixtures, had been repurposed or rebuilt from scrap. But the room also hummed with quiet intensity. Mr Fassal motioned towards two young men. 'Ms Mordwell,' he said, beaming with pride, 'I present to you our CerebroNet hunters—Hiro and Diego.'

Ms Mordwell surveyed the young men before her. Diego stood motionless, his face a blank canvas. Hiro twitched, barely containing his fury, veins pulsing at his temples as if readying to twist themselves into knots. Ms Mordwell's smile widened. 'I am delighted to meet you,' she said, her soft voice cutting through the tension in the room.

Hiro responded only with a glacial stare.

Diego began to respond, the words teetering on the edge of his tongue, when he felt Hiro kick his ankle. Diego's cheeks flushed a deep red. His eyes darted away from the others. He opened his mouth, but no words came out. Instead, he pressed his lips together and hung his head, letting the silence stretch on.

Ms Mordwell noticed the kick. Her smile morphed into a cryptic grin as she turned her full attention to Hiro, meeting his intense gaze. 'Your reputation precedes you. Word of your impressive skills has travelled wide. I'm sure your parents are very proud. Just like Mr Fassal.'

Hiro's reply was a venomous hiss: 'My parents are dead, and the words of an enemy hold no value for me.'

Mr Fassal's face flushed bright red, his eyes igniting with fury. But before he could chastise Hiro, Ms Mordwell made a swift, placating hand movement. The commanding gesture extinguished Mr Fassal's rising temper like a bucket of ice water.

It took him just a couple of seconds to regain his composure. When he spoke, Mr Fassal emphasised the words with a deliberate pause to stress the unspoken significance: 'The enemy... of our enemy... is... our friend.'

Ms Mordwell smiled. 'Your healthy scepticism is a good survival tool in our world, Hiro. While our paths and pasts may differ, we share a common goal of defeating the real enemy—CerebroNet.'

Diego's lips pressed into a thin line. Ms Mordwell's words seeped into his mind, and subconsciously, he agreed. He nodded, just a fraction of an inch, so subtle it might have gone unnoticed by anyone not paying close attention.

Hiro's expression transformed from a scowl to a mocking smirk. He lifted his hands in a grand, theatrical gesture, his voice dripping with sarcasm. 'What's this? Has the tide turned between you and the machine? Weren't you once inseparable champions of the bionic evolution of humanity?' He tilted his head, pretending to be confused. 'What caused this sudden change of heart? What could CerebroNet have done to fall from your grace?'

Ms Mordwell chuckled in response. 'Sudden change of heart?' The sound of her laughter reverberated throughout the room. 'I've been against CerebroNet since its beginning. Look at me.' She gestured across her augmented body. 'This is the result of CerebroNet's reckless experiments with fusion reactors and clandestine technologies.'

The room fell silent as she closed her eyes, lost in a moment of painful recollection. When she spoke again, a slight tremor crept into her voice. 'Yes, I cannot be against technology. After CerebroNet's reactor exploded, my body was wrecked. Most of me is technology now.' Her eyes filled with sincerity, and her facial muscles relaxed. 'And even being half-machine, what do you think would happen to me if I were to remove the ID implant to avoid CerebroNet's control?' Ms Mordwell looked deep into Hiro's eyes, then into Diego's. 'I, just like anyone else, would be kicked out of New London. Discarded like worthless rubbish.'

Hiro's eyes sparked with satisfaction and, for a moment, danced between Diego and Mr Fassal before resting back on Ms Mordwell. Then, brimming with resentment, he said, 'So, in your eyes, we are all just rubbish.'

Ms Mordwell gave him a stern look, and her voice took on a sharp, disapproving tone. 'You know that's not what I meant.' She locked eyes with Hiro. 'With all my cybernetic enhancements, I would not be welcome among you. I doubt even the Cybergangs would open their arms to an ex-New Londoner.'

'There! You've got it right. You're not welcome here,' Hiro exclaimed, provoking a series of angry huffs from Mr Fassal.

Ms Mordwell's eyes flickered, acknowledging Hiro's hostile demeanour, but she chose not to engage. Instead, she turned her head slightly, her gaze drifting past him and settling on a point in the distance. For a moment, she seemed lost in thought, her mind wandering to a place far beyond the confines of the room. As she refocused her attention, she drew in a slow, steady breath. When she parted her lips to speak again, her words flowed with a deliberate calmness, each one measured and even. The earlier traces of emotion in her voice had vanished, replaced by a controlled, almost detached tone. 'CerebroNet has pitted all of us against each other. This division is our greatest weakness and its greatest strength. Please think for a moment. Technology, in itself, is not bad. It's all about how it's applied, and in CerebroNet's case, it's outright evil.'

Mr Fassal's eyes flicked back and forth between Hiro and Diego, studying the micro-expressions on their faces. When Ms Mordwell made her point, he turned his attention to Diego. 'Your last encounter with CerebroNet turned almost deadly. You were fortunate to escape alive, weren't you?'

Diego's chiselled features hardened. His eyes dulled, and he lowered them. His long lashes shrouded his gaze as he studied the worn leather of his boots for a moment. When he spoke, his voice sounded fragile. 'Yes, we narrowly made it,' he said, the admission seeming to catch in his throat.

As Diego voiced his admission, Hiro felt the weight of guilt settle into his chest, squeezing the air from his lungs. His breath hitched as a knot of remorse constricted his throat.

Ms Mordwell noticed the slight change in Hiro's demeanour. 'I'm very sorry you had to experience that. But I am afraid things will only get worse. I realise you don't want to listen to me. I know I'm not welcome here. But I am risking my life because I need to warn you.' Ms Mordwell fell silent, her expression turning sombre. She closed her eyes and reached up to massage her right temple. A moment passed before she opened her eyes again, piercing Hiro with an intense gaze. 'The government has again partnered up with CerebroNet. They are building a fleet of military droids. Their intent is, and I quote, "to cleanse the city of Technophobe vermin". The military droids will also raid neighbouring cities for resources. They are already building them.' She eased herself into a chair by the rusty conference table. Everyone watched her, wide-eyed. After a brief pause, she continued. 'I am sure you've heard about people disappearing without a trace.'

Diego nodded. 'Yes, Clara's son has vanished. There have been stories about people disappearing for a long time now.'

'I am afraid these are not random disappearances,' Ms Mordwell continued. 'You see, to build an army of military droids is too expensive, so the government has authorised CerebroNet to produce more droids using augmentations. You understand they are taking people from your communities. To them, anyone without an ID implant is expendable. Just a biological device.'

Mr Fassal's brows knitted in plain agitation. 'What are you saying? What are they doing to our people?'

Ms Mordwell paused as if gathering the strength to articulate the next horrifying fact. 'The people that CerebroNet snatches are being dissected and converted into military augments—soldiers stripped of will, desire, or self-control. Once transformed, they become mere pawns in CerebroNet's plan to wipe out

Technophobe communities off the face of the Earth. You will all be destroyed by the husks of your own people.'

A long, grave silence spread like a shroud, swallowing the room whole.

Ms Mordwell turned towards Hiro and said, 'CerebroNet is already too powerful, thanks to its nefarious pyrozetton. But with an army of controllable, augmented humans, it will become unstoppable. That will be disastrous for all of us. I'm aware of only some of their plans, but I already know that people on both sides of the city will suffer. It might be the last thing humanity witnesses before the wipeout.'

Hiro looked worried. 'What is pyrozetton?'

'It is a device. A technology that gives CerebroNet its computing power. Something almost otherworldly that cemented its dominion over society.' She paused, letting her words sink in. 'The only path to salvation, to free the world from CerebroNet and rebuild our society, is to obliterate CerebroNet. And to do that, pyrozetton, the heart of CerebroNet's superintelligence, must be ripped out and destroyed.'

Diego raised his hands in despair. 'But what can we possibly do about it? Our weapons are not even effective against a single Eyeball. There are thousands of them. And now there is an army of zombie droids? What should we do? Throw sticks and rocks at them?'

Ms Mordwell stood up, her figure casting a long shadow over the table. 'We must bridge our differences and collaborate to stand a chance against the government and CerebroNet. I am training a group of elite agents to sabotage their plans. Topple these autocratic usurpers. Rebuild our government so each faction of our society is represented fairly and equally. My super-agents are trained to be everything in one: warriors, scientists, spies. Everything they might need to locate the pyrozetton and destroy it.'

Several moments passed in silent reflection. Ms Mordwell studied Hiro and Diego, gauging their reactions. 'Join me. We don't have much time. My training programme is rigorous, but it will prepare you for all the challenges ahead. It will help you to defeat CerebroNet. You will become instrumental in building a fair society for everyone.'

A sarcastic laugh escaped Hiro's lips. 'And naturally, we must be implanted with your tech for the training to work.'

'Yes. It's a tiny neural interface that will enable access to the training simulator. We must use the enemy's tools against them. You use your analogue technology against CerebroNet's droids, don't you? This is no different. It's what you're good at.'

Hiro recoiled as if her words were physical blows. His expression twisted into a storm of anger. 'No different!'

Mr Fassal intervened to stop Hiro from erupting. 'Those analogue tools don't do you any good any more. You were lucky not to kill yourself and Diego. What will you do against a military android? Think! We have an opportunity to get rid of CerebroNet and rebuild our communities.'

Hiro erupted in a guttural roar that reverberated through the room. 'This is madness! You two are just power-hungry opportunists, ready to sacrifice anyone. For even just a taste of power.' He locked eyes with Mr Fassal, his gaze burning with disappointment. 'How can you even contemplate cooperating with this abomination and be okay with us being turned into cyborgs? Really? You're a traitor!'

Mr Fassal's face turned almost purple. Veins bulged on his forehead. His whole body trembled as he struggled to contain the fury bubbling beneath the surface. 'How dare you call me a traitor?'

Ms Mordwell placed a reassuring hand on Mr Fassal's shoulder. Her gaze met his with layers of unspoken empathy.

Mr Fassal felt a little ashamed of his reaction. The embarrassment extinguished most of his anger. He nodded, forced a smile, and gestured towards the exit. 'Shall we?' Then he gave Hiro a murderous stare. 'We'll continue this conversation later.'

Before Ms Mordwell turned to leave, she addressed Hiro once more. 'Your youthful idealism is beautiful but also limiting.' She extended a small device towards Hiro.

Hiro glanced at her hand but stood still, ignoring the device.

Ms Mordwell exhaled. 'Don't be so stubborn.' She put the device on the table. 'This tool will give you a tactical advantage next time you deal with the Eyeballs. It will slow them down.'

Hiro looked at the device again. 'You think your little toys will make me change my mind?'

Ms Mordwell smiled sadly. 'I do hope you will reconsider.

For all our sakes.'

As Mr Fassal and Ms Mordwell left, Hiro stormed out of the room without saying a word to Diego.

Diego picked up the device from the table. It was a small, translucent cube with an interplay of shimmering, holographic circuitry inside. He marvelled at its pulsating core for a moment, then put it in his pocket.

* * *

Hiro and Diego sat across from each other in silence. The door burst open, causing Diego to jump.

Mr Fassal's hulking figure squeezed into the tiny room. The bulging veins were gone from his forehead. His face wasn't purple with anger any more. But Hiro knew rage still possessed Mr Fassal, so he didn't even turn to look at him. Instead, he continued to look straight at Diego with pursed lips.

'You ungrateful little shit,' Mr Fassal growled in a voice as harsh and biting as frost. 'Have the decency to respect the hand that feeds you. I plucked you from the gutter, and this is how you repay me?'

Heat crept up Hiro's neck, searing his cheeks, but he swallowed a nasty retort.

Mr Fassal didn't expect a reply. He just continued. 'It seems you think you know everything, that you can judge everyone. Fine. But it also means you don't need my babysitting. I expect you to settle your debt tonight.'

Diego's eyes widened at the impossible deadline. He opened his mouth, wanting to negotiate. But before he could utter a word, Mr Fassal screamed, 'And if you can't... get the fuck out of here!'

With his heart pounding in his chest and adrenaline surging through his veins, Hiro resisted the temptation to voice his thoughts. He remained silent as the feeling of helplessness engulfed him.

Mr Fassal's gaze narrowed. Before storming out, he said, 'Make sure you take advantage of Ms Mordwell's gift. I don't need your excuses or your corpses. I need the rent you owe me.'

* * *

The last few mentally and physically exhausting days had drained Hiro and Diego. They moved at a sluggish pace, as if burdened by heavy weights. As they neared the Thames, powerful gusts of wind brought a mix of overpowering odours.

The Thames's murky waters served as Old Town's sewage and waste dumping ground. But the river always repaid the favour. It regurgitated the filth in an unending cycle of floods. The flood zone became a vast barren wasteland marking a nauseating boundary between Old Town and New London.

Hiro and Diego had long grown accustomed to the smell of decomposing humanity. However, the sharp sting of ammonia had always jolted them into newfound focus.

'I can't believe he kicked us out. You'd think he'd be on our side,' Diego grumbled.

Hiro replied after a moment of silence. 'Not that you leapt to defend me.'

Diego stopped. 'Defend you? They were the ones under attack, not you. You jumped in like a mean teenager from the get-go.'

Hiro's patience teetered on a knife-edge. 'What did you expect? Did you want me to volunteer for augmentation? Become a fucked-up mix of man and machine?'

'I didn't say th—'

'If you want to, go. Join her. Do it. Leave me alone.'

'No, I don't want to join her. But you didn't have to be an arse about it. A simple "thank you, no" would've sufficed. What did you achieve? Look at us now, back in the fucking ruins. My body is still in agony from yesterday's adventures.'

With his energy reserves almost depleted, Hiro felt too exhausted to engage in another fight. To de-escalate, he forced composure into his voice and explained. 'Calm down, mate. Either way, we're stuck hunting an Eyeball. We'd still be here, wading through shit, no matter what I said. If we hunt down an Eyeball, we'll score ID spoofers and a roof over our heads, with or without Fassal.'

Hiro's last word had barely left his tongue when a sound shivered through the gloom behind them. As if synchronised, Hiro and Diego spun on their heels. The sight of CerebroNet's Eyeball froze them mid-motion.

Hiro stared at it with an unblinking gaze. A blue aura that enveloped the droid pulsated like the heart of a crazy beast. The hole in the Eyeball's shell, a result of Hiro's attack with a rust-eaten rebar the day before, bubbled a viscous, fluorescent-green substance.

The Eyeball didn't zap them. It hovered in place, bobbing ever so slightly up and down.

Hiro held his breath and whispered 'It's the same one.'

Hiro's mind grappled with a frantic dilemma—fight or flight. Fleeing was pointless, and fighting under the circumstances was ludicrous. And yet, amidst the madness, he gravitated towards the ludicrous. And for that, he needed his EMP net.

Hiro's hand inched towards the backpack slung over his shoulder. When his fingers brushed the strap, the droid blared a high-pitched warning. Then it darted its round body closer to Hiro's face.

Observing Hiro's move, Diego understood the plan, and his heartbeat resonated throughout his entire body. With sweat dampening his brow, he ventured to move his arm behind Hiro, away from the Eyeball's sight. He moved his fingers to unzip Hiro's backpack.

The Eyeball let out the same ear-splitting sound. It zipped to Diego's side with a speed that forced him to stumble backwards. Then the Eyeball retreated, leaving some distance between itself and them. It used the space to project a hologram.

'What the fuck?' Diego muttered in disbelief. 'Is it trying to communicate with us?'

A deep furrow appeared on Hiro's forehead. His mind wrestled with the unprecedented situation. 'They don't communicate. They zap.'

The pixelated hologram flickered and stuttered. Its accompanying sound oscillated between muffled whispers and tinny echoes, punctuated by sporadic clicks. The incomprehensible footage, taken from an aerial perspective, showed two figures engaged in conversation. Their faces and voices were indecipherable through the digital corruption.

The content of the enigmatic footage held little interest for Hiro and Diego. However, the peculiar behaviour of the Eyeball freaked them out. Neither knew what to do about it. The Eyeball's anomalous conduct had spanned two odd encounters. Something was wrong with it. Bewildered, they exchanged an uneasy glance. It appeared the Eyeball demanded attention by imposing its incomprehensible hologram upon them. Hiro had an anxious thought. He began to wonder if the Eyeball's erratic behaviour stemmed from a malfunction of Mr Fassal's ID spoofers.

A second Eyeball zoomed past. It noticed the trio beneath and, as if defying the law of inertia, veered towards them with a swift change in direction. Upon approaching, it scanned Hiro and Diego, emitting the characteristic electronic sounds.

The colour drained from Diego's face, leaving him swaying on his feet. He whispered, 'I feel sick.'

The damaged Eyeball stopped the hologram playback as the

new arrival halted beside it. The air filled with a chorus of electronic chatter. It would probably sound like a heated discussion if humans could understand the ultrasonic communication between the CerebroNet droids. But Hiro's and Diego's ears could only perceive the byproduct of the Eyeballs' chitchat: a series of rapid electronic clicks and whistling sounds.

Whatever the broken Eyeball said prompted diagnostics through optical imaging by its counterpart. A sequence of fast light pulses marked the end of the scan. These flashes overwrote the damaged Eyeball's protocols and redirected its information flow. The broken Eyeball initiated its emergency procedures. Its blue shimmering disappeared as haphazardly blinking yellow lights replaced it. It jerked upwards and glided away towards New London.

The remaining Eyeball started another scan on Diego. This time, it was much longer and seemingly more thorough. While the droid was busy with Diego, Hiro, avoiding sudden movements, took off his backpack. He unzipped it. But before he could retrieve the EMP net, the Eyeball finished scanning Diego and refocused its scan on Hiro. Hiro slowly passed the bag to Diego.

From the corner of his mouth, Hiro instructed, 'Use the EMP.'

As panic coursed through Diego, his palms grew damp with sweat. His voice trembled as he blurted out, 'It's digging into our IDs.' He reached into his pocket. His hand closed around Ms Mordwell's translucent cube. Her words resonated in his head—it will slow them down. Diego pulled out the cube and, before Hiro could voice his protest, pressed the glowing circle on the cube's surface. The pulsating core turned bright red. Uncertain of what would happen next, Diego hurled the cube toward the Eyeball.

Wide-eyed, Hiro watched the cube whizzing through the air. The scene seemed to unfold in slow motion. A comet trail of bright red light marked the cube's path. With a soft thud, the gadget landed behind the Eyeball.

Hiro and Diego froze.

Nothing happened.

As the Eyeball completed its scan, it shot skywards and disappeared from view.

Hiro turned to face Diego with an expression full of genuine bewilderment. 'Why did you do that?' he asked.

Gasping for air, Diego bent over, gripping his knees. 'I don't know,' he gasped in a shaky voice. 'I panicked, I thought... I thought it would freeze for a while or something.'

Hiro forced a calm tone. 'Well, at least we know it's useless.'

Before Diego could reply, two quadcopter drones appeared overhead. Black as coal, they glistened under the setting sun, looking like oversized dragonflies. The quadcopters had teardrop-shaped bodies, wings in tandem configuration, and a sensor array instead of an insect's head. The drones circled in the air with their sensors and cameras pointed at Hiro and Diego. Without a doubt, they were the primary subjects of surveillance.

With a burst of noise and a storm of dust, two military-style vans skidded to a stop nearby. The sight of armed men leaping out from the vehicles sent a jolt through Hiro. The men looked ready for combat. Each was geared up with a variety of weaponry. The ease with which they wore their equipment suggested a deep-rooted familiarity. They moved as a unit, like a well-oiled machine on a predetermined path. That path was leading straight towards Hiro and Diego. As the dust settled and the unit moved closer, Hiro's initial assessment wavered. These weren't soldiers. Hiro could make out an unsettling detail—every one of them had fire tattooed on their faces. This was a Cybergang.

Hiro had had his fair share of encounters with Cybergangs. His contraband sales of the drone engines' organic components had led to many clandestine transactions with Cybergangs. Each meeting was also an opportunity to observe the evolving tapestry of their tattoos. Each member wore them with pride and defiance. Cybergang tattoos were more than just ink on the skin. They were allegiance badges, intimidation tools, and personal journey markers. They signified rites of passage, hard-earned victories, and commitments to their gang. Hiro remembered a few designs: a fallen king symbolising lost leadership, a thorn crest representing resilience in adversity, and a shattered chain denoting liberation from norms.

But the tattoos of this Cybergang were unique. These tattoos had a vitality that set them apart from anything Hiro had seen before. They pulsed with otherworldly hues and moved with creepy shadows. With each step, they shifted and transformed. It was a terrifying spectacle. To Hiro, it looked like these were not tattoos but entities from hell superimposed on their faces. They lived, breathed, and morphed into devilish masks of threatening horror.

Their leader stood out. His face tattoo was a canvas of bright dancing flames. The effect was sinister, making him appear demonic. The leader tapped something on his wrist, and a projection of Hiro's face appeared in front of the gang. Muttering something inaudible, the leader raised his hand. A finger extended, pointing at Hiro.

Diego's instincts to protect Hiro kicked in. He grabbed the backpack and fumbled inside it. His fingers wrapped around the EMP net launcher. But just as he was about to aim, one of the gang members moved. In a flash of blinding light, an energy beam shot from his weapon. A jolt of energy travelled through Diego's body. He stiffened for a second. His muscles began twitching with involuntary spasms. The EMP launcher slipped from his grasp. His paralysed body gave way to the effects of gravity, sending him crumpling to the ground.

Hiro dropped to his knees to help Diego, but found himself powerless to do anything meaningful. His heart pounded as he watched Diego convulsing. The gang closed in. Hiro's mind raced. Shivering from adrenaline-fuelled panic, Hiro reacted. He snatched the EMP launcher and fired. Hiro's aim was true. The net flew straight towards the leader and enveloped his flame-adorned face. When Hiro pressed the trigger once more, an EMP surged right into the leader's head.

The discharge sent the gang leader's implants into disarray. His tattoos flickered like broken neon lights before fading away. His massive body faltered, succumbing to an unexpected stupor. Just as he was about to fall backwards, his mates' arms wrapped around him, preventing him from hitting the ground.

The absence of augmentation inputs wrecked the leader's abilities. His hands quivered. Desperate to reactivate his augmentations, he frantically poked at his arm display. The pained expression on his face subsided, and the leader attempted to regain his footing. His legs trembled, hardly supporting him. With a glance at his crew, the leader had a revenge plan ready. A tone of menace touched his shaky voice when he spoke. 'We weren't told to bring him in alive, were we?'

The Cybergang members encircled Hiro and Diego. With a smirk, the leader reached behind his back. The setting sun glinted off a metal object as he pulled it into view. His knuckles whitened as his grip tightened around the metal baseball bat's handle. The corners of his mouth curled up in a grin. The gang leader swung the bat with a force that made the air whistle.

Hiro only just registered the incoming blow before it connected with his face. A sickening crunch accompanied the jaw-shattering impact. Hiro's teeth and blood flew from his mouth. The droplets sprayed outward, tracing arcs in the air before staining the ground. Hiro collapsed. Blood gushed from his mouth, and his teeth lay scattered around him.

Diego tried to push himself up. He wanted to get to Hiro, but his paralysed muscles prevented him from moving. Diego felt locked within his own body, his eyes glued to the unfolding scene of horror. He wished he could close his eyes or blink away the sight. But he couldn't move. The scene that he was forced to witness felt more painful than the physical pain he was enduring from the blast of the energy weapon.

United in a single-minded rage, the gang circled Hiro. Each member itched with the desire to transform Hiro's body into a bloody piece of meat. Some were hitting him with baseball bats, and others relied on the weight of their boots. Their frenzied blows landed with crunching thuds, each one sending shockwaves through Diego's body. After a while, some of the Cybergang members grew tired and stepped back, watching as the remaining members continued their assault on Hiro's body.

In an instant, the violence came to an abrupt stop as the Cybergang members collapsed, their bodies writhing in intense spasms and their grunts filling the air.

As if in answer to his unspoken question, an Eyeball descended from the darkening sky. It had returned. The shimmering blue light still engulfed its pierced composite metal body as it hovered above Hiro.

* * *

Hiro felt her touch, the gentle force of his mother's slender fingers against his back. Her palm radiated warmth, and a sense of safety emanated from her touch. Nestled against her chest, the rhythmic beating of her heart resonated against his cheek. Each thump lulled him further into tranquillity. A familiar scent enveloped him. The comforting aroma of his mother—a blend of lavender and the earthy warmth of freshly baked bread. The scent danced around him, swirling into a cocoon of reassurance. It grounded him with a deep sense of belonging. He raised his gaze to relish the gentle curve of his mother's smile and the radiance of her skin. As his eyes focused, a gasp clawed at his throat.

Instead of his mother's face, Hiro was looking at a metallic skeleton soaked in crimson. Blood dripped from the robot's face as a monstrous grin stretched across it. The robot began to rock Hiro. A chilling echo of his name bounced off the hollow metallic interior, 'Hiro. Hiro...' The voice grew into a shriek. An insidious dread overpowered Hiro. A tidal wave of loneliness washed over him, drowning him in despair and helplessness. His limbs grew heavy, weighed down by invisible chains. Shadows crept closer. The surroundings blurred and shrank.

With a harsh gasp, Hiro jolted awake. His heart pounded like a drum against his ribs. A figure stood next to him. Caught in a fog of confusion, Hiro's mind struggled to place the familiar face beside him. Gradually, recognition dawned upon him. It filled him with relief. It was Diego, his trusted friend.

Diego's lips moved. Hiro focused his attention, trying to tune into Diego's words. Slowly, the words began to make sense, and a smile spread across Hiro's face, a genuine feeling of connection washing over him. He managed a reply, 'Let me sleep, bastard.'

Hiro reached to push Diego away and froze mid-action. A robotic arm with streamlined metallic bones encased in translucent skin stretched out from his body. Hiro moved his arm. The robotic arm responded. It glided, mirroring his intention. Hiro clenched the hand into a fist. The artificially jointed metallic fingers came alive with a mesmerising display of tiny, flickering lights. Hiro struggled to grasp the unfolding scene. Suspecting his senses were playing tricks on him, Hiro lifted his other arm. To his profound astonishment, his other arm displayed the same features.

'I am still asleep,' he said matter-of-factly. 'I need to wake up.' But the words of his friend shattered his hopes.

Tears cascaded down Diego's cheeks as he whispered, almost inaudibly, 'You are awake.' Overwhelmed with emotion, Diego's body shook with sobs. His eyes, filled with nervous energy, darted across Hiro's face. Diego bowed his head and murmured, 'I am so sorry.'

Time appeared to crawl as Hiro's mind scrambled to comprehend this new reality. He brought his hand closer to his face. His eyes traced the intricate rotations and articulations of the fingers. For a moment, he marvelled at the delicate precision and fluidity of the mechanical movements. He studied each joint and digit as if trying to decipher their workings.

As the realisation descended on Hiro, he looked at his torso and ripped off his hospital gown. A wave of bewilderment washed over him, freezing his facial expression in a state of disbelief. His eyes widened, and his mouth fell slightly agape. He was looking at the aftermath of the brutal attack. His eyes traced the contours of his body, most of which was covered with transparent synthetic skin, seamlessly merged with his remaining dark skin. He studied the network of intricate devices nestled within him. The second wave of realisation felt like a punch to his guts. 'Oh shit… This can't be permanent,' he whispered as if trying to convince himself. Hiro hesitated before reaching to touch his face. When his fingertips made contact, he retracted his hand as if it gave him an electric shock.

Hiro's eyes grew wide. He turned to face Diego. 'Tell them to take all this off of me.'

Diego's voice quivered. 'You've sustained horrendous injuries, Hiro. Your bones and organs were almost obliterated. Healing naturally wasn't an option.' Diego paused. 'You nearly died.'

For an eternal moment, Hiro fixed his gaze on Diego. 'But they'll eventually remove all this, right?'

'They saved your life, Hiro. Your doctor says with some physio and training, you will have no changes to your lifestyle.' Diego swallowed. 'Once fully recovered, you'll feel and look just like a normal human.'

Hiro's face contorted into a grimace. 'Like a normal human?' He looked down at his body again and shouted, 'Are you fucking insane?' He was hyperventilating between his yells. 'No changes to my life? Look at me. Look! Do you see what they've done to me?'

Diego cried.

Hiro wept, too. After a moment, he whispered, 'Why didn't you protect me? How could you let them do this to me? I trusted you.' Hiro felt cold sweat forming on his back. He felt dizzy, and his vision became blurry. Intense pain enveloped him, overpowering his senses as flashes of bloodied boots and the sickening sound of crushing bones rumbled through his consciousness. 'I'd rather be dead than this,' he whispered. Hiro's hands trembled as he covered his face and let out a soul-wrenching scream.

CHAPTER 3

Hiro stirred in the hospital bed. His dream dissipated as a soft light seeped through the semi-opaque smartglass wall. The glass provided a serene barrier between his secluded tranquillity and the hustle and bustle beyond.

Hiro's state was delicate. The moment he opened his eyes, the room itself seemed to mock him. Everything was too clean, too composed. The interior walls were seamless white panels, glowing with a soft, clinical light that tried—and failed—to be calming. There wasn't a scuff, a crack, a loose cable in sight; nothing for his gaze to snag on except perfection.

A slow, shifting panel of digital art pulsed across one wall: abstract shapes dissolving into one another, colours sliding from muted blues to warm ambers and back again. Every few seconds, the image tried to guess his mood and adjust—calmer, softer, more pastoral—until Hiro wanted to rip it down just to make it stop trying to please him. Below it, a thin strip of text blinked gentle health metrics in pastel fonts, as if his vital signs were part of the decor.

The air was scrubbed and filtered to the point of unreality, scented with the faint, synthetic tang of disinfectant and something floral that had never grown in soil. A climate unit purred invisibly behind the walls, keeping the temperature at a perfectly neutral level that still managed to feel wrong on his skin. The bed beneath him adjusted to every twitch, its smartfoam reshaping itself, refusing to let him even be uncomfortable on his own terms.

The most trivial things set his teeth on edge: a faint holographic hospital logo hovering near the door, slowly rotating; the rhythmic blink of a status light over the ceiling track. And, worst of all, the outer wall of the room—a sheet of smartglass—with a small vent window perched high on it, far beyond reach: the only true opening to the outside. Its very existence felt like a personal insult—too small, impractical, teasing. A potential gate to real air he could see but never touch.

The day had started on a sour note. Yet as the moments passed, the sharp edge of his anger dulled, worn down by the room's relentless, artificial calm. A wave of indifference washed over Hiro. He realised the day's course mattered little to him, if at all.

With a resigned sigh, he pushed against the crisp hospital sheets and sat up. His movement triggered the smartglass into action. With a melodic hum, the opacity of the glass decreased. Reaching full transparency, it revealed the grand spectacle beyond.

The awe-inspiring panorama stretched out before Hiro. A golden bath of sunlight amplified the view's shimmering brilliance. From the ruins of Old Town, reborn like a phoenix from the ashes, stood New London, nested under its colossal protective dome atop a hill. The dome, made of countless transparent triangles, their edges glinting under the sun's rays, shielded the city from the harsh elements. Architecture, boasting adaptive facades, glistened in the sunlight. Silver hyper-loop channels interlaced the cityscape, their burnished tubes glinting like strands of metallic yarn woven into the urban tapestry. Courier drones darted and twisted among the hyper-loop conduits, their intricate movements sketching chaotic patterns against the azure backdrop of the sky. The city streets hummed with a vibrant dance of intertwined technology and people.

Everything looked and felt different here. No one bothered with clunky analogue tech. Instead, the crisscrossing streamchain networks enveloped this half of London in their digital embrace. Hiro imagined invisible threads pulsating with data. He pictured them as veins joining the city and its inhabitants into a colossal creature.

As he watched the buzzing city, his awe of the sprawling spectacle gradually melted away. A swelling tide of bitterness and repulsion replaced his awe. Hiro realised this intricate urban ballet was orchestrated by the same pervasive super-intelligence that he despised with every iota of his essence. The realisation left him feeling even more isolated and disconnected from the vibrant life unfolding outside his window.

The gentle whoosh of the opening door shattered Hiro's bitter solitude. He wiped his eyes. His fingers registered the contact and the wetness on his cheeks, but it felt as if someone else had touched him.

A woman with a smile as dazzling as a supernova approached his bedside. 'Hello, Hiro,' she said in a honeyed tone. 'I'm your doctor. My name is Dr Yashi Patel. Can you share with me how you're feeling today?'

Dr Patel was the weirdest fusion of human and robot Hiro had ever seen. Her head, with a face full of human emotion, had been affixed to a mechanised torso. The torso mimicked the structure of an upside-down cockroach. Her arms, two slender, metallic manipulators, were centred beneath her collarbones. Below them, several pairs of folded medical instruments were arranged all the way down her belly, like the delicate legs of an insect. The instruments twitched as if ready to spring into action at any moment. The torso, a sleek expanse of polished metal, was anchored to a slender pole outfitted with two robust wheels that lent her mobility.

Normally, Hiro would feel a profound sense of vulnerability and a sharp pang of embarrassment at exposing his tears to a stranger. But Dr Patel's freakish appearance left him confused and filled with apprehension. This cocktail of revulsion and confusion cemented his tongue to the roof of his mouth. He could only stare, trapped in mute turmoil.

Unfazed by his stillness, Dr Patel smiled. 'Let's evaluate your recovery process.'

With a silent whirr, a set of scanners unfolded from her back like wings, stretching over Hiro. Dr Patel wheeled alongside his bed, methodically scanning his entire body. Once done, a holographic projection sprang up from her abdomen. The image portrayed a detailed rendition of Hiro's anatomy, overlaid with a dynamic canvas of blinking lights, cryptic symbols, and scrolling lines of text. Dr Patel sifted through the imagery, assessing each of Hiro's augmentations.

Dr Patel's gaze jumped between different sections of the hologram. 'You spent eight days in surgery. Your recovery is nothing short of miraculous. We expected the medibot to keep you in an induced coma for another month, at least.'

'You mean you didn't expect it to switch me on?'

Dr Patel's expression morphed into a compassionate smile. 'I know how bizarre this must feel. After accidents like this, despite medibot's cerebral trauma therapy, patients often take some time to adjust to such drastic transformations.'

'This wasn't an accident!'

Dr Patel nodded. Her features softened even more. 'What matters, Hiro, is that you survived and are well.' She paused, allowing the weight of her words to sink in. 'Your brain has recovered. The new neural interface allows direct communication with AIs, manipulation of virtual worlds, and even connection with other neural interfaces. Your augmented vision will let you perceive infrared and ultraviolet in the augmented reality overlays.' She motioned to Hiro's torso. 'Inside, a fleet of nanobots is working diligently, acting as your enhanced immune system.'

Dr Patel retracted her wing-like scanners, folding them behind her back. 'Your medibot is currently undergoing unscheduled maintenance. But once your rehabilitation programme is complete, your synthskin will be activated to mimic your natural skin tone. You will be in full control of all your augmentations. And you'll regain your agility.'

Hiro scrutinised Dr Patel's face. He had so much to say about all this, but his thoughts tangled into a bowl of mental spaghetti. He stayed quiet.

Unruffled by his angry stare, Dr Patel said, 'Rest assured, Hiro, you're in the best hands. By the time you're discharged, you'll feel strong.' She gestured with her thin metallic hand, and the hologram of his internals dissolved into nothingness. 'I'll discuss your rehabilitation plan with your boyfriend.'

Hiro's eyebrow shot up in confusion. 'Boyfriend?'

'Yes. With the support of your loved ones, your recovery will be even smoother.' With that, she swept out of the room, leaving Hiro alone to grapple with his new existence.

* * *

Hiro's knees trembled, threatening to give out at any second. His shoulders rolled out of sync with his flailing arms. His entire body jerked, mimicking a poorly controlled marionette under the capricious command of an unseen puppeteer. The struggle to keep his balance was draining. It siphoned away his minuscule energy reserve. Despite this, Hiro pushed ahead.

With a pneumatic hiss of the sliding door, Dr Patel and Diego entered Hiro's room. The sight before them provoked a startled gasp from the doctor, and her fingers darted across the air.

Puzzled, Diego shouted, 'What the fuck are you doing?'

Informed by Dr Patel's silent alert, two hospital guards stormed into the room. As they bypassed Diego and the doctor, their objective immediately became apparent.

Hiro was attempting to squeeze himself into the tiny window on the smartglass wall. His body twitched. Akin to an unsteady pendulum, one leg twitched and kicked at the air, a spasmodic attempt to find momentum. His shaky platform comprised a chair balanced atop a small coffee table, which in turn teetered on a cabinet.

The guards held Hiro steady while Dr Patel activated a medication dispenser, delivering a mild sedative. As his shaking subsided, the guards extricated him from the hazardous position and moved him onto the bed. Once the furniture was repositioned, they retreated at the doctor's nod.

Diego sat on the edge of Hiro's bed with an expression of disbelief. 'You can barely move. What was that all about? Why?'

Dr Patel's expression hardened. 'Hiro, your wellbeing is of utmost importance to me. You can talk to me about anything. Even your suicidal thoughts.'

'I was trying to escape. Not kill myself,' Hiro shot back, a hint of bitterness coating his words. He gestured around the room with a sweeping motion of his hand. 'I can't pay for all this. And I won't become your servant robot either.'

Dr Patel appeared taken aback but quickly regained her composure. 'Patients with PTSD often experience confusion,' she began, carefully choosing her words. 'But you must know there is no reason for worry. Your treatment has been paid for. Actually—' She paused, checking the records in the data stream. 'You have an open account.'

The puzzled expressions on Hiro and Diego's faces confused Dr Patel. She glanced back at the patient file. Satisfied with the correctness of her data, she studied their faces for a while, trying to decipher the reason behind their perplexed reaction. 'All necessary documentation and payments were processed before your arrival at the hospital. That is a fact.'

Diego shifted uncomfortably. 'This must be a mistake.'

Hiro dug an elbow into Diego's ribs to get his attention, but Hiro's face did the real talking. His eyebrows shot up, eyes almost popping from their sockets as his lips vanished, thinning into a bloodless white slash. Perhaps, to Dr Patel, Hiro's expression looked ridiculous, but to Diego, it was a sign written in flashing neon—shut the fuck up!

Diego turned back to Dr Patel. 'I mean, everything is in order. Right?'

Sensing their persistent disbelief, Dr Patel felt she ought to explain. 'Before your arrival, CerebroNet provided us with your complete medical history and extensive scans of your injuries. An open credit line. And most importantly, bags of your plasma. Given your rare blood type, we would not have been able to synthesise it in time. Without it, your survival would have been uncertain. Because of your employer's swift actions, we programmed the surgeon bot. It was ready to operate on you before you even arrived.'

She paused, letting her words sink in, then added, 'The CerebroNet corporation always takes good care of its employees, but this... this was an exceptional response. Storing your plasma and authorising your employer to act in an emergency was a very wise decision.'

Silence spread through the room. Hiro and Diego sat, stunned, staring at Dr Patel.

'Now,' Dr Patel concluded in a softer tone, 'I must insist you rest. Any further strain could hinder your recovery. Don't hesitate to ask me for anything you need. Please, Hiro. I mean it. And try to conserve energy for your upcoming physiotherapy. The sessions will start in a couple of days.'

Finished with her explanations, Dr Patel rolled out of the

room with a low hum of her wheels, leaving Hiro and Diego in contemplative silence.

As twilight melted into darkness, Hiro turned on a desk lamp. Its gentle luminescence painted a complex tapestry of shadows across the room. Still bewildered, he studied the shadows absentmindedly, then hoisted himself up and looked at Diego. With a confused look on his face, he began following a mental thread.

'I hunt CerebroNet's Eyeballs. Strip them down and sell the parts to the Cybergangs. I am the only one who could supply them on a regular basis. Cybergangs need the parts to make and sell Leviathan. Leviathan sales make up the majority of their income.'

'If not the only source,' interjected Diego.

'Right. Yet, the Cybergang wanted to kill me. On the other hand—CerebroNet, being an evil artificial super-intelligence, becomes my saviour. Somehow, it has in its possession bags of my apparently very rare plasma, which it managed to send to the hospital before I died. And if that is not fucked up enough, CerebroNet pays for all my surgeries and all these shitty implants.'

Lost in contemplation, Diego fixed his gaze on the sprawling lights of the New London skyline. Without taking his eyes away from the sight, he said, 'It looks like it paid for my stay here as well. I was treated when we arrived. I was given water, food, and a room to sleep while I was waiting for your recovery. They never asked me to pay for anything.'

Hiro nodded as if Diego's revelation added gravity to his swirling thoughts. 'Hmm, okay,' he said and fell silent for a long moment. 'So, my dear friend, could you try to answer this for me? Has Dr Patel been liberal with her drugs, and am I tripping? Or am I still concussed and hallucinating?'

Diego giggled. 'Probably the first one. But no, all this is fucked up.'

Hiro massaged his temples to soothe his confusion. 'Nothing makes sense.'

After another moment of quiet, Diego admitted, 'Sorry, man, the more I think about it, the less it adds up.'

Hiro sighed. 'Yeah, it doesn't. Listen. About yesterday.' He squinted at the memory. 'I wasn't fair. I was...' He paused. 'An arsehole. I shouldn't have taken it out on you. I'm sorry. Please don't be mad at me.'

Diego smiled, his dimples catching the warm glow of the desk lamp. 'Don't worry about it. Who wouldn't freak out?'

'Thank you. Anyhow, there is one thing we are certain about, right?' Hiro smiled. 'You're my boyfriend.'

The room erupted with Diego's laughter. 'They kept asking if I was family.'

'Well, you are. You are my only family,' Hiro said, his voice soft with sincerity.

'And you're mine,' Diego replied, reaching out to Hiro and enveloping him in a tight hug. 'I was terrified of losing you. Cybernetics or not, I'm so grateful you're still here.' He paused, a twinkle in his eye. 'Well, even if in fragmented pieces.'

Hiro laughed at that, playfully shoving Diego away.

'You're a jerk.'

'Guilty as charged.'

'But you're my jerk,' Hiro said. Then his tone shifted, suddenly serious. 'There's no need to pretend that nothing has changed. My life will never be the same because I am not the same any longer. But let's use this situation to our advantage. Suppose, as a boyfriend, you're upset that I listed CerebroNet as my emergency contact instead of you. Create a scene. Try to dig for more information about CerebroNet's involvement from the doctor. How it got hold of my blood, why it paid, and anything else you can find out.'

Diego nodded. 'It's a shot in the dark, though. And she's scary.'

Hiro grimaced. 'Don't be a pussy.'

'Meow,' replied Diego, and they both laughed.

Diego stood up. 'I guess we have nothing to lose.' He looked at Hiro with a commanding stare. 'Rest now. And remember—no more stupid escapades.'

Diego made his way to Dr Patel's office. His mind swirled with potential arguments and pleas. He didn't have a concrete plan. But his raw emotions would fuel his improvisation. He was no stranger to painful feelings when it came to Hiro. The sting of jealousy was all too familiar to Diego, flaring up anew with each fleeting romance Hiro sparked with the women of their community.

Having spent countless days pacing these paths, Diego navigated the maze of hospital corridors with ease. Dr Patel's office came into sight with its glass walls turned opaque for privacy. A faint red cross pulsed rhythmically as he neared the door. Diego accepted it as an indication of her unavailability and waited. He had a favourite waiting spot. It served as his sanctuary, his retreat during daylight hours as he loyally awaited Hiro's recovery. His self-designated post had a tropical plant that stood in striking splendour. He always loved learning about Earth as it once was and telling Hiro stories about his discoveries of animals and plants of the past. This was the second substantial plant he had ever encountered. The first was a desiccated specimen in an abandoned building. This one had a rich, earthy smell, contrasting sharply with the hospital's sterile scent.

With no chance to return to their previous lives, the hospital had unwittingly adopted Diego as a transient resident. The enormity of the hospital held a peculiar allure for him. A myriad of strangers flowed in and out in a constant stream. They bore little resemblance in their behaviour and physical appearance to the individuals of his community. The soft shuffling of their footsteps and murmuring voices became a persistent, calming background noise to his otherwise tumultuous thoughts. Diego watched these weird and fascinating lives pass by, well aware he would have to learn how to live among these people in New London and use technology if he was to stay by Hiro's side. He would need to support Hiro in adjusting to his new life. Diego reckoned it would be a Herculean task.

Diego waited, trapped in the stillness of the passing of time. Seconds congealed into minutes, minutes stretched into hours, but it didn't faze him. He needed answers. The involvement of CerebroNet terrified him. He was determined to give the performance of his life to get more information from Dr Patel. His fingers, nails bitten short, mindlessly picked at his cuticles as if attempting to rip away his thoughts about theattack and CerebroNet.

Diego began to wonder if Dr Patel would be back at all. He wanted to ask the receptionist, but he was somewhat afraid of it. The receptionist robot was shrouded in the metallic sheen of cold, calculated precision. It had a face that held only a ghostly imprint of human features. Diego didn't know whether it was an intentional design or a reflection of New London's desire to keep the gap between humans and machines. He wondered if the robots shared a dislike for the corrosive rains that killed the plants. But his thoughts screeched to a halt as his eyes locked onto a group of men exiting the gravity lift. They approached the receptionist robot—tattoos, alive with flames, dancing across their faces with every movement.

Diego felt chilling tendrils of fear give way to a potent dose of adrenaline. It yanked him out of his petrified stupor. In a flash, he spun on his heels, which squeaked on the sterilised floor.

Bursting into Hiro's room, Diego's words erupted from his mouth like a siren, 'They're here! We need to get out!'

Hiro jumped up in his bed, recognising the terror etched onto Diego's face—a grotesque portrait painted with strokes of raw fear that signalled one thing: they were in a sea of new troubles.

'Who?' Hiro demanded, already swinging his legs over the edge of his bed.

'The Cybergang! The ones with flames on their faces!'

The colour drained from Hiro's face as a wave of shock made him dizzy. He sat down and murmured, 'How did they find us?' Hiro didn't know if he still had a real, beating heart, but it felt like it was plummeting in his chest. He felt Diego's hands on his shoulders, and the world tilted as his friend's face blurred as it grew distant. A loud popping sound rang out, followed by a sharp sting on his cheek—a slap that jolted him back to reality.

The ringing in his ear faded, and Diego's urgent voice came through, 'We need to move. Do you hear me? We must move,' Diego repeated, his voice trembling with desperation as he violently shook Hiro's shoulders.

Hiro blinked the haze away, and the panic kicked back in. He pushed Diego away. 'But where to?'

In response, Diego's eyes darted around the room, scanning every inch as if looking for an invisible thread of hope. The room, once a sanctuary, became a prison. He glanced at the small window and immediately disregarded it He approached the door, fear lining his every move. With a trembling hand, he pressed the access panel to open it. He peered into the corridor. There were no Cybergang members in sight. But, in Diego's estimation, it was only a matter of seconds before they would stop talking to the receptionist bot and descend on them.

Diego looked at Hiro, assessing whether, being medicated, he was alert enough for their escape attempt.

Still dazed but clearly reading the situation and Diego's facial expression, Hiro said, 'I can do it.'

Diego swallowed hard, his throat bobbing like a cork in rough water. Then, grabbing Hiro's hand with a steel grip, he pulled him into the corridor, heading away from the reception towards another set of gravity lifts. Ahead, a nightmare came to life. More flame-adorned faces stepped out from the belly of the lift.

Diego's hand moved like a lightning bolt. His fingers jabbed at the first access panel within his reach. A wave of relief washed over him as the door slid open with a gentle hiss. Wasting not a moment, Diego shoved Hiro inside. Hiro staggered, barely managing to stay upright. Diego pressed on the access panel. The low hiss of the door sealing them off was the only disruption in the otherwise lethal silence that engulfed the room. Their newfound sanctuary mirrored Hiro's hospital room. A man lay asleep in bed. His surroundings were aglow with the luminous colours of holographic flowers and balloons decorated with cheerful messages.

A wheelchair rested next to the bed, hinting at the inhabitant's limited mobility. Diego signalled for silence. He navigated the room with movements as quiet as a ghost's whisper. He took the patient's clothes and threw them at Hiro. Then Diego went back to the door. He pressed his ear against it, attempting to gauge what was unfolding outside. He was met with nothing but silence. For a second, he wondered whether that was because no one was on the other side of the door or if it was impenetrable to sound. A feeling of unease gripped Diego as he considered the probability of the Cybergang's pursuit. He was certain that they would not be satisfied with Hiro's absence for long.

Diego retrieved the holographic balloons and flowers from the bed and pressed them into Hiro's grasp. 'These should obscure our faces,' he whispered.

Hiro seemed trapped in a world of slow motion, much to Diego's dismay. So Diego adjusted the plan. He manoeuvred the wheelchair behind Hiro and pushed him into it. After summoning his courage, he opened the door and peered outside. A group of Cybergang members still congregated by the distant lift. Diego's only option was to brave the journey through the reception, hoping the first group had left.

Diego pushed the wheelchair forward. Hiro veiled his face behind the bouquet. Diego hid in the cloud of balloons. As they moved past reception, they witnessed a disturbing sight. Towering Cybergang members surrounded the robot receptionist. Its connection to the network had been severed, rendering it a prisoner of the unfolding chaos. Its neon-green eyes flickered, trapped in a loop of augmented reality torture. The robot convulsed. Its movements grew more erratic as its artificial synapses were deliberately snapped, one after the other.

Diego attempted to ignore the horrific scene unfolding in front of him. He continued to push the wheelchair towards the lift as the cluster of jostling balloons obscured his face. Every muscle in his body screamed for him to run. Despite this, he maintained a steady walk while waging a fierce internal battle against his primal instinct. They reached the lift, and Diego pressed the button. He was determined not to glance back. To maintain the facade of an ordinary hospital scenario.

The lift doors slid open with no interruption from behind. Diego wheeled Hiro in. He selected the ground floor and risked a last glance towards the reception as the doors began to close.

The Cybergang leader's tattooed face stared back with a suspicious look. Recognition dawned in his eyes. Just before the doors closed, the flames lunged forward.

Diego wheeled Hiro through the hospital's bustling vestibule and plunged them into the city's streets, teeming with a blend of humans and androids. Diego spotted a group of Cybergang members rushing through the crowds towards the hospital and sprang into action. He tore the holographic bouquet and balloons from Hiro's hands and pressed them into the hands of a confused passer-by.

Glancing around, Diego's gaze landed on a narrow passageway obscured by shadows. He helped Hiro out of the wheelchair and pulled him into the passageway.

A familiar, ominous hum echoed from above, the aerial whisper of Cybergang drones invading the sky. A few minutes separated them from the unforgiving sweep of the drones' relentless scanners.

They hurried forward. As they rounded a corner, Diego

skidded to a halt. His breath hitched. A sheer, unscalable wall loomed before them. A dead end. He ran towards it, his heart pounding like a frantic metronome when the truth sank in.

Seized by a sense of impending doom, Diego turned back. Fuelled by stress and Dr Patel's drugs, Hiro was faltering. He made a weird, repetitive gesture with his new arms. Diego interpreted it as waving for him to go ahead without waiting.

Then Hiro yelled, 'Go. Find a place to hide. I'm right behind.'

Diego banged on the closed doors of restaurants and shops. Their apathetic greeting robots uttered pre-recorded advertisements, oblivious to his spiralling panic. Diego found an old utility door. Its rustic lock had the battle scars of time and corrosive rain. Despite Hiro's best efforts to ram the door, the lock remained defiant.

Frustrated, Diego knocked down an unfortunate greeting bot. He viciously twisted one of its limbs until it snapped free with a dull cracking sound. He hammered the obstinate lock with the severed arm until it gave in.

Diego raced back and clasped Hiro's arm, pulling him into the dark room. Hiro's legs faltered as he crossed the threshold, sending him crashing onto the hard floor. With a swift movement, Diego slammed the door shut before their hideaway was noticed. As the door closed, a cloak of darkness enveloped them. The only sound that disturbed the echo of the slammed door was the sound of them gulping in the stale air.

Relief washed over Diego as he heard the shuffling sound of

Hiro finding his footing and rising. This black void allowed them to let their adrenaline levels subside and gave them time to figure out their next move.

A flash of blinding white light erupted before them. The powerful glare hurt their retinas. Hiro and Diego shielded their eyes with their hands. They blinked rapidly, attempting to blink away the lingering afterimages. Gradually, their sight returned, revealing the dark, circular mouth of an energy gun aimed at them.

CHAPTER 4

The buzz of the weapon powering up sent Hiro and Diego into a hasty retreat until they found themselves backed against the cold wall.

Recent battles, narrow escapes, and brushes with death had profoundly chipped away at Hiro's resilience. The cumulative toll of these ordeals had left him teetering on the edge. At that moment, the harsh metallic glint of the gun became the proverbial last straw. He gave up. His legs folded beneath him, and he sank to the floor like a puppet with severed strings.

Diego's eyes darted about like a spooked cat, searching for an escape. The threat of the weapon limited their options. Deciding that engaging with their captor was the safest approach, Diego raised his hands in a universal gesture of surrender. 'We mean no harm,' he announced, forcing a smile.

It was humanoid, modelled after a young woman. The robot's beauty, though clearly crafted, was striking and radiated allure. Its dark blue lips exquisitely contrasted with the pristine white of its synthskin. The fembot ignored Diego while its azure eyes assessed Hiro from beneath a platinum-blonde fringe.

Diego shifted from one foot to the other. 'Don't worry, we are unarmed,' he clarified, attempting to engage it in conversation.

The fembot's gaze shifted to Diego. Her blue pupils expanded as they assessed him, her shoulder-length synthetic hair moving with synchronised fluidity. Diego felt like he was under an intense, penetrating scan. When the robot spoke, her tone was unexpectedly mature, clashing with her youthful appearance. 'No shit. If you were, you would already be dead.'

Diego stood speechless. His eyes widened in disbelief. His mouth moved as if trying to respond. Yet no words came.

When Hiro was in the coma, Diego immersed himself in deciphering the enigmas of the new world into which life had unceremoniously plunged him. He witnessed the daily life of New London unfold before him. Through these observations, he realised its realities were vastly different from the narratives imprinted on him since his youth. Diego buried himself in troves of information about New London's history, traditions, and regulations. He deduced that the Technophobes' accounts of New London and its inhabitants were only partially accurate. The rest were twisted into propaganda to reinforce the Technophobe doctrine. Contrary to the teachings, the robots of New London were engineered for courtesy and compliance. He discovered that the cornerstone of autonomous technology design was the No Harm Directive, which would incapacitate any robot that posed a threat to humans. The robots he encountered at the hospital were nothing like the nasty machines demonised in Technophobe lore. But not this one. The fembot threatened them with a charged weapon, violating that fundamental principle. On top of that, it seemed to mock them.

Before Diego could vocalise his thoughts, the fembot nonchalantly pointed her gun at the deflated Hiro, who slumped on the floor at an odd angle. 'What the fuck is wrong with this one? He looks ridden hard and put away wet. But a scan of his systems indicates optimal performance. Is his biological component broken?'

Diego's mouth fell open, and he blinked rapidly. It took him a long moment to regain focus. He chose to offer a plausible response without revealing too many details. 'He's just tired. We needed a brief break. We're leaving now. I'm sorry for the intrusion. I thought this place was unoccupied.'

As Diego finished the sentence, the distinctive hum of Cybergang drones seeped into the room from outside. The sound instantly captured the robot's attention.

Diego's gaze darted towards the exit. His eyes widened, and his lips tightened in a thinly veiled attempt to mask his rising panic.

The robot curled her blue lips into a mocking sneer. 'Let me guess. Those are your pals outside, looking for you.' The fembot moved a few steps closer to the door. She wasn't even trying to mask her sarcasm. 'I guess they're here to help you since you're all so tired. Let me call them in for you.'

Diego's voice wobbled under the pressure of his lie. 'No, please. Just let us stay here a bit longer. We'll be out of your way in a moment.'

'Like hell you will,' the fembot replied. 'You're dumb to cross the Cybergangs. They won't stop until they've hunted you down. Tell me who you are and what you're doing here, and I might consider letting you catch your breath here. Otherwise, feel free to go back outside.'

Hiro lifted his eyes, studying the artificial features for a moment. 'We didn't cross any of the Cybergangs. We never even dealt with the one with flames. They keep coming after us, and we don't know why.' He summoned his remaining energy and forced himself back to his feet. 'They already killed me once. Thanks to them, I became nothing but worthless augmented junk.' Hiro steadied himself and looked the robot in the eye. 'I don't care who finishes the job. You or them. I'm too fucking tired to care. Do your worst.'

The robot's grin disappeared. 'What do you mean by "flamed"? What does this Cybergang look like?'

Hiro and Diego stared at the robot for a while, perplexed by the odd question.

'Like all Cybergangs. Not at all nice or lovely, you know. These ones have live tattoos. Fire on their faces.' Diego said.

The robot's eyes glinted. 'Now listen. I'll make you a deal. I'll help you escape the Cybergang if you help me first.'

Hiro sighed. In an exhausted voice, he asked, 'What do you want?'

'My scans show you have nice tech in you. Your human component is broken, but your tech works fine. I need to use it,' the robot replied.

Confusion wrinkled Hiro's forehead. 'Use my implants?' Hiro blinked at her in silence for a moment. 'I can't help you. I know nothing about these augmentations or how to use them.'

'Chillax. I'll tell you what to do. Are you in or are you out?'

Hiro turned to Diego, who responded with a helpless shrug.

'Perhaps it's best if you rejoin your friends outside,' the fembot offered, prodding them towards the exit with the gun.

Hiro conceded, 'Okay, okay. We're in. What do you need me to do?'

The robot holstered her gun and went to the door. She attached a device to the doorframe. With a soft click, a shimmering force field sprang to life. 'This will buy us some time. Do you have names?'

'Diego.'

'Hiro. And you?'

'Call me Gia. Now, come with me.'

Guided by Gia, they embarked on a journey into the depths

of the building. They navigated a labyrinth of immense rooms connected by laser-cut holes in the walls.

Often, they would descend a dusty flight of stairs. The steps appeared to have been unused for a very long time. Sometimes, they used a ladder to descend into another void cut into the floor.

Emerging from another hole, they found themselves in a vast, cavernous space unlike anything Hiro or Diego had ever seen. They paused, trying to take in the scope of the room with its enormous monoliths. The towering shapes disappeared into the shadowy ceiling high above. Hiro craned his neck, but he couldn't see their peaks. Each formation was perfectly rectangular. They stood in endless rows like silent sentinels, spaced symmetrically throughout the room. Hiro didn't know the purpose of the monoliths, but they made him feel small.

A network of organic-looking tubes linked each monolith. To Hiro and Diego, the sight was alien. They followed Gia, feeling a mix of awe and dread. Occasionally, some of the towers would spring to life with a loud hum, and a symphony of colourful lights would burst into a dance all over the structures. Gia navigated the maze with a confidence that suggested she was oblivious to the hum and the lights. Hiro and Diego exchanged anxious glances but stayed silent, letting their footsteps echo in the darkness.

They approached another laser-cut gap in the wall. It was barely large enough for a person to fit through. Gia dropped to her knees without a word and crawled through the opening. After exchanging more confused glances, Hiro and Diego followed her.

The wall turned out to be awfully thick, making the hole into a narrow, suffocating tunnel. Their elbows, knees, and shoulders scraped against the sharp, chipped stone. The air, heavy with the scent of damp concrete, grew thinner with each laboured breath.

When the tunnel spat them out into a yawning void, its vastness dwarfed them. A soft, shifting, ethereal glow saturated the room, making it feel like they had crossed the threshold into a mystical realm. Nothing about this place resembled a human construction. They struggled to process the surreal beauty surrounding them. Giant orbs floated in the air, their luminescence giving them an almost magical quality. Diego wondered if they had entered an art installation. Light beams crisscrossed the room, creating intricate, shimmering connections between the orbs. The walls, lined with a dark material, pulsed with ripples of sizzling energy that seemed to originate from random points. The waves intersected and created mesmerising patterns before fading away, only to be replaced by new designs. Hiro and Diego stood transfixed, the unfolding spectacle holding them in a hypnotic grip. Despite their uncertain circumstances, the serene ambience, the soft shimmer of light, and the gentle, rhythmic hum of the surrounding machinery instilled a sense of calm.

Gia gestured to a meticulously crafted hole in the concrete floor. It held a delicate cluster of filaments at its centre, alive with a dance of colourful lights. The exposed network throbbed rhythmically, a symphony of data in motion. Hiro felt a twinge of apprehension as he noticed that the filaments beat in synchrony with the colossal spheres surrounding them.

Resting beside the opening was an unassuming black box. Its sole distinctive feature was a sturdy cable that anchored it to the radiant bundle of filaments. The cable appeared to be alive. Like a vital artery, it pulsed with lights from the data stream, creating a mesmerising aura of energy as it channelled data from the throbbing cluster into the box.

'That's my fried workstation,' Gia said, her voice adopting a patient, explanatory tone as she pointed towards the box. 'Without it, I can't sift through the stream flowing through these server nodes.' She gestured towards the orbs. 'I need more processing power to filter the data, select the right stream, and inject my Seekers.' She then turned her gaze to Hiro, adding, 'This is where you come in.'

Shifting her focus to Diego, Gia issued her next set of instructions. 'Your job is to keep watch over the tunnel we just crawled through. Stay alert and let us know if you detect any movement or sound on the other side.'

Diego stepped forward, curiosity piqued by the box and the knot of filaments. 'Did you say you're injecting your Seekers? You're infecting the data stream, aren't you?'

'I'm contributing to it,' Gia said coolly, her blue eyes locking with Diego's. 'I'm not questioning why you're wandering around with a spoofed ID, am I?'

Diego felt warmth rush to his face. He lowered his gaze and

murmured, 'Fair enough.'

Satisfied that she had quelled any further objections from her new accomplices, Gia declared, 'Okay, let's do it so we can get the fuck out of here.'

Hiro placed a reassuring hand on Diego's shoulder, their eyes locking in a shared understanding forged through years of trials and tribulations. To an outsider, their expressions might have seemed inscrutable. But to them, it was as clear as day. With a nod, they reached a wordless agreement.

Hiro's eyes stayed with him as Diego disappeared into the tunnel. Then he gestured at the throbbing filaments in the floor's opening. 'What do you expect me to do?'

'I just transmitted the filter parameters and my code to your neural interface,' Gia replied, focusing on her damaged workstation. Gia disconnected the thick cord linking the box to the pulsating mass of filaments. A port opened above her wrist, and she plugged it in. 'I will decrypt the stream. You need to hold and filter it, inject my seekers, and pass it back to me for re-encryption. That's it. Once we're done, we leave.'

A wave of embarrassment washed over Hiro, fuelled by his total lack of understanding. He swallowed hard, his voice trembling as he stammered, 'I... I don't know what any of that means. What am I supposed to hold? What filters?'

Gia paused. Her earnest gaze fixed on Hiro as if she was trying to piece together a puzzle. Her blue eyes flickered, and her robotic face precisely mimicked an expression of astonishment.

'What do you mean?'

Hiro's face contorted, caught in a turbulent dance of frustration and helplessness. His heart raced from the absurdity of the situation. He didn't want to be anywhere close to this nonsense. But he needed to participate in this so they could escape the Cybergang, even as the tech jargon of the robot swirled around him in mockery. It was all too much. His throat tightened. In a crackling voice, he blurted out, 'I am a Technophobe.'

As Gia assessed the utter absurdity of the statement, her disbelief grew almost palpable. She threw her hands up in exasperation. 'Are you fucking kidding me?' she yelled.

'Yeah, you know…' Hiro's voice trailed off. A hint of sheepishness crept in as he felt a tide of self-consciousness pull him under. 'We… we don't engage with tech all that much.'

'A Technophobic cyborg? This is ridiculous!' she exclaimed, burying her face in her palms.

'I never wanted to become an augment. The Cybergang turned me into a pile of meat, and when I regained consciousness, I found myself pieced together with all these implants. Before I had a chance to figure out how to use all of this,' he gestured across his body, 'the Cybergang was after me again and chased us from the hospital.'

Gia's frustration seemed to diminish. 'The same Cybergang?' she asked with a hint of concern in her voice.

'Yes,' Hiro confirmed. 'The same fire faces.'

A strange, robotic emotion flickered across Gia's face. After a brief pause, she composed herself and addressed Hiro again. Her tone was more serious. 'Okay, I'll need to access your systems to set the filters. You need to enable access for me. I've sent a request to your interface. Did you get it?'

Hiro hesitated. 'I think so. Something is blinking in my eye.'

'Okay, then open it and accept.'

An awkward admission fell from his lips, 'I don't know how.'

Gia sighed. Then she rifled through her workstation, extracted another cable, and handed one end to Hiro. 'Let's do it the old-fashioned way.'

Hiro regarded the cable as Gia instructed him to plug it into the port behind his ear, demonstrating with her own port.

A look of disgust washed over Hiro's face. 'I don't want to plug anything into me.'

Gia eyed Hiro again, contemplating whether her endeavours were in vain. Yet, she knew she had committed too much to walk away. 'Forget that Technophobe nonsense. That's just a load of bullshit that doesn't even apply to you anymore.' She paused to let her words sink in. 'Yes, the past got you this far. Yes, it made you. But it doesn't matter what you are made of. The only thing that matters is what you do from now on. Embrace the change as evolution, or you will destroy yourself and everyone around you.'

Gia extended the other end of the cable towards him.

He hesitated, his eyes darting towards the tunnel where Diego stood guard. At that moment, the reality of their situation recrystallised in Hiro's mind. He couldn't let Diego confront the

Cybergang again. Not after what he'd put him through. Taking a deep breath, he touched the skin behind his ear and felt it give way to reveal a port. He took the cable from Gia and plugged it into his head.

Gia connected the other end of the cable to the port behind her ear. Almost instantly, Hiro felt a surprising surge of reassurance wash over him. It was as if Gia's strong, confident presence had somehow transmitted itself through the cable. It fortified him with a sense of determination he hadn't felt in a very long time.

'Brace yourself. I will request SuperUser access to your systems,' Gia warned in a calm but firm voice. 'You're going to be inundated with critical warnings. You need to approve them all. Just follow the prompts that will appear in your mind's eye.'

As Gia had warned, Hiro's vision was soon swamped with a barrage of flashing alerts. A wave of discomfort rippled through him as he realised his mind was linked to a computer. Among everything else, it also felt like an invasion of his privacy.

'We're racing against the clock here. You need to pull yourself together,' Gia urged, jabbing him in the chest to emphasise her point.

Snapping out of his stupor, Hiro began to acknowledge the slew of warnings. All were cautioning him about the perils of granting SuperUser access to his systems. It was a surreal experience. He had never before interacted with technology through the power of thought. But he found it surprisingly intuitive. Then, his entire field of vision was consumed by a final, all-encompassing warning, which bathed everything in a red glow. A stark white message appeared over the sinister backdrop. A voice echoed in Hiro's ear: 'Sharing SU key may result in loss of system controls.' The options 'Decline' and 'Share SU Key' pulsated before him. Casting one last glance at the tunnel, Hiro took a deep breath and shared the key. His vision immediately flooded with streams of code and terminal inputs, a digital maelstrom that confused and overwhelmed him.

'Holy shit!' Gia exclaimed, snapping Hiro back to attention. 'How did you get all this? This is unbelievable!' She stared at Hiro, her gaze distant, as though she were looking through him. Her hands and fingers manipulated the air in front of him, interacting with something invisible. Still looking through him, she asked the strangest question Hiro had ever heard. 'What are you?'

Before he could react, Diego's yell cut through the air as he ran towards them. 'They're coming!'

'Damn it!' Gia exclaimed, her attention split between juggling the relentless flood of data overwhelming her senses and the imminent danger closing in on them. Her sharp and authoritative voice sliced through the tension as she issued a rapid set of commands to Diego. 'Climb through the tunnel at the opposite end of the room. Go downstairs and open the utility hole. Wait for us there. We're almost done.'

As Diego sprinted away, the room came alive with the deep hum of a drone. Hiro followed its ascent, its vibrations pulsating through the air and reverberating off the enormous orbs. Time seemed to stretch as the drone paused mid-air. A wave of nausea washed over Hiro as he realised it was aiming at them. Without a second thought, he hurled himself at Gia, sending them spiralling towards the ground.

A cocktail of confusion and fury flickered across Gia's face. She had interpreted Hiro's move as an assault. Her hand shot out to snap his neck in the chaos of their descent. But as her workstation erupted in a hailstorm of sparks and debris from the drone's onslaught, she grasped that he had just saved her. They hit the ground with a jarring thud, Hiro pinned atop Gia. Wasting no time, she shoved him off and seized him by the collar, hauling him to his feet. 'Run!' she roared, the drone's shots snapping at their heels.

Gia yanked Hiro down a narrow staircase into a cramped chamber flanked by two corroded metal doors on the opposing wall. Ignoring the doors, she pulled Hiro towards the centre of the room. Diego was on his knees, struggling to pry open the ages-old lid of a utility hole.

'I can't open it!' Diego screamed in exasperation.

Gia shoved Diego away and slipped her slender finger into the crevice of the thick steel lid. She hooked it and slid it aside.

A pungent stench attacked their nostrils.

'Get in!' Gia barked at Hiro, the command reverberating in the confined space.

Hiro hesitated. His eyes darted between the utility hole and

Gia. Noticing her stern expression, he realised she wasn't open to discussion. He lowered himself onto the cold concrete and extended a leg into the abyss.

Gia shoved his other leg, forcing him to descend until he stood in the murky sludge. 'Get on your knees and crawl right,' Gia instructed. Seizing Diego's arm, she yanked him towards the opening. 'Make sure he keeps moving.'

Diego dropped to his knees beside the utility hole, placing a hand on Hiro's shoulder and locking eyes with him. 'We have to move,' he implored in a soft but urgent tone. Casting a final glance at Gia, Hiro vanished into the void, Diego trailing behind.

Gia descended next. She dragged the manhole cover back overhead just as the rumbling from above intensified. She extracted her laser gun and traced it along the seam between the lid and the frame, welding it shut.

With Gia's harsh commands echoing around them in the pipe, they pushed forward through the filth. The thick, suffocating stench of human waste seemed to morph into a malevolent entity from the depths of hell. It enveloped them, a tangible, suffocating presence that clawed at their throats and began to shred their sanity.

'Faster!' Gia's voice echoed down the pipe as her portable light cast looming shadows ahead of them. 'The tide is coming in. It will overflow the Old Town's sewage system and fill this pipe with crap. You'll drown in the shit of your fellow Technophobes. Is this how you imagined you'd die?'

Gia only heard a 'nuh-uh' from both humans as they crawled onwards even faster.

They entered a much larger pipe with similar openings on its sides. Each spewed waste into a central pool of human excrement. Gia ordered them to jump. Hiro and Diego held their breath, then plunged into the putrid soup of sewage.

Gia pointed ahead. 'We need to keep moving.'

Their journey through the sea of waste descended into a living nightmare. Trudging through the sludge was like battling wet concrete—every step demanded a Herculean effort. With each passing moment, fatigue weighed heavier on them. It felt like the sludge itself conspired to hinder their progress, thickening with every step.

The odour was a physical presence, suffocating and all-encompassing. Yet, as the miles wore on, the stench seemed to retreat. Not because it diminished, but because their senses dulled under the relentless assault.

Gia's voice bounced off the tunnel walls as she called out, 'Almost there!' She extended her arm. Her finger aimed at a distant, faint outline—a vertical ladder swallowed by the inky blackness.

As they approached the ladder, the sludge grew heavier, pulling at Hiro's legs like quicksand. It seemed to rise and thicken with every step. Hiro's new legs failed him, and he felt the cold filth close over his head.

Diego and Gia fought to free Hiro from the sludge's viscous grip, but their efforts were as fruitless as trying to wrestle an oil-slicked snake.

Gia threw herself into the muck. Using the pipe's floor for leverage, she hoisted Hiro up like a barbell. Gasping for breath, Hiro clawed at the ladder's rungs, hauling himself up. Diego and Gia followed.

Exhausted, covered in filth, and trembling from the ordeal, they stumbled into a vast network of passageways. It was a relic of the city's once thriving underground transport system. They trudged behind Gia, their footsteps echoing off the walls. Time lost meaning as they navigated a maze of ladders and twisted tunnels. Breathless and coated in filth, they stepped into a large concrete room.

A solitary, flickering light cast long shadows on the floor. At the opposite end stood a rusted metal door. A fat pipe snaked along the far wall.

Gia shattered the silence. 'Welcome home.' She tossed her weapons into a corner before issuing one last command: 'Strip off.'

It sounded more like an ultimatum than a request. Hiro's eyebrows shot up in surprise. A flash of defiance crossed his eyes. He and Diego exchanged a wordless glance. Getting naked in front of a robotic woman wasn't a situation either of them had anticipated.

Hiro opened his mouth as if to protest, but snapped it shut as Gia pointed her index finger at his face. 'Make no mistake, guys, you're not stepping foot inside if you are trailing shit behind you.' She took off her top and flung it into the corner. Her trousers followed suit, coming off with the same ruthless efficiency. Completely naked, she turned to face them. 'Before you begin, check your pockets. Trust me, you don't want to be fishing for valuables from your shit-soaked clothes once you're squeaky clean.'

Gia gripped a retro-style wheel fitted to the pipe and cranked open the valve with a deliberate twist. A forceful torrent of water surged from an overhead spout. A big blue grin spread across her face. She extended her arm, palm up, and fluttered her fingers in an inviting motion, encouraging the humans to join her.

Hiro and Diego took in the sight of Gia, noting the precise anatomical design of her body, as the gushing water removed the dirt from her pale synthskin and platinum-blonde hair.

Diego, a man with nothing to lose and nothing in his pockets, discarded all his clothing in the same dirty pile. He joined Gia under the waterfall, allowing the robust stream to cleanse the stubborn filth stuck to him.

Hiro lingered in the corner. The hospital getaway seemed like a distant memory, almost as if years had passed since. Despite feeling drained, he mustered the strength to peel off his shirt. After a moment's hesitation, he turned his back and reluctantly took off his trousers, adding them to the growing heap of discarded clothes. His heart pounded as he observed Gia and Diego from the corner of his eye. They ignored him, enjoying the waterfall. He approached them with deliberate steps. Wincing, he subjected himself to the water's icy embrace. Despite his shyness, Hiro lost himself in sensation, feeling the difference between his synthetic and natural skin. His synthetic flesh tingled with an electric buzz, each nerve ending playing a heightened rush of sensation. The coolness seemed to seep deeper into his synthetic layers, creating a unique and unsettling feeling that both intrigued and unnerved him. When he looked up, he found Gia's gaze fixed on him. She was assessing his body.

'I see you haven't adjusted your synthskin colour. But don't worry, I will help you match it to your beautiful dark skin tone,' she said. Her eyes slid up and down his body before fixating on his privates. 'Looks like the medics were determined to save some of the original parts. It's nice to know your medibot appreciates the classics. Isn't it? I hope all the functionality has also been restored.' A slight smile and a wink accompanied her words.

Despite the freezing water, Hiro felt a hot flash spread all over his body. His face turned red, and he turned away.

'Hang on, you haven't sealed your data port!' Gia's laugh cut through his embarrassment. 'It needs a good clean. Come, let me help.'

She turned him around by his shoulders. Hiro tensed—but then found himself captivated by the intense blue of Gia's eyes. She held his chin with one hand while her other pressed against his forehead. She tilted his head, exposing the data port to the stream. Once satisfied, she straightened his head and tapped behind his ear to seal the port. Gia scanned Hiro from head to toe before shifting her gaze to Diego. Diego had stepped out of the waterfall and was trying to shake off the excess water from his hair.

'Now, your inspection, sir. Turn around for me,' she chuckled.

Diego extended his arms sideways and spun around, proudly displaying his clean body.

'You aren't shy at all, are you? Anyhow, we're all ready for a hot shower and soap,' she declared with apparent satisfaction.

After turning the wheel to stop the stream, she headed towards the door and paused in front of the scanner. The door obeyed, revealing a bright, spacious room beyond.

'Come. Follow me.'

CHAPTER 5

The hot shower had washed away the remaining grime and the shock of their narrow escape. Freshly clothed, Diego buzzed with renewed vigour. Within the security of Gia's hideout, he was a bubble of excitement. He trailed her every move, captivated by the holograms that responded to her touch. Just as he became talkative when nervous, Diego also chattered when excited. Animated by a cocktail of adrenaline and curiosity, he fired off a cascade of questions: he wanted to know what the huge floating orbs were, how the holographic displays worked, and what the shimmering protective field around her consoles was. Navigating the flickering panels, Gia offered explanations with the patience of a robot.

Hiro, in contrast, remained silent. He was pleased only with the clean clothes, not just for their freshness, but for how they covered the sections of his synthskin that didn't match his dark complexion. He knew it was irrational, but he felt embarrassed in the presence of this flawless robot. The metallic bones and blinking devices beneath his transparent synthskin made him feel ashamed, then angry with himself for feeling that way. The cleansing shower hadn't re-energised him as it had Diego. Still fatigued, he couldn't shield himself from the intrusive thoughts that spiralled around him like a constrictor, squeezing tighter with every breath. Watching Diego and Gia, Hiro felt like a pariah among them. This was his first day as an augmented human outside his sterile hospital room, but this brave new world had already eroded his meagre will to live. Never before had he felt so vulnerable being naked in front of Diego. But at that moment, he saw himself as a misfit. He wasn't entirely human any longer, nor was he a robot. He wished all these absurd thoughts and emotions would cease forever. Hiro wanted to be alone. He wanted to crawl under a rock and stay there until he died.

As the last display flickered to life, Gia turned to a concealed compartment nestled within the wall. She slipped her hand inside and, with a practised motion, retrieved an object and handed it to Hiro.

His hand recoiled as a jolt of terror shot through him the moment he recognised the object. It was a data cable similar to the one she had connected to his data port. His heart pounded, his face twisting into an expression of dread. 'What's this for?'

'Don't freak out, man,' Gia said, her voice full of excitement. 'I stumbled upon something in the data stream. The Cybergang was on our heels. I didn't have time to inspect the find. So, I archived the lot and saved it inside you just before the drone started shooting at us.'

A cold, sickening wave of disgust flooded Hiro. He stiffened, his entire body recoiling from itself. 'You saved what inside me?'

'Everything,' Gia replied matter-of-factly. 'I archived the whole lot.'

'You can't just... You should have asked me first!'

Gia shrugged. 'Time wasn't on our side, was it? Anyway, all the data was saved way too fast for its size. I'm not sure if the operation was successful. Anyway, relax. It's just archived data. It's harmless.'

Hiro's face contorted into a grimace of repulsion, and his breaths sped up to desperate gasps as his body began trembling with uncontrollable rage. 'Don't you think I should decide what is or isn't harmless for me? You used me as a hard drive. I'm not some fucking piece of machinery like you!' Seized by a sudden surge of anguish, Hiro jumped up from the seat, his hands grasping his head, fingers clawing into his hair before curling into tight fists. 'I didn't sign up for any of this. I am not a machine.' He began pacing around the room. 'I am not a fucking robot!' he yelled, consumed by the unhinged outburst.

Unfazed, Gia returned his anger with an impassive stare.

'What's wrong with you? Calm down, human. You definitely aren't a robot. If a robot had this kind of fit, it'd be scrapped.'

Hiro continued lashing out at Gia. 'You used me. You're no better than CerebroNet. Stripping us of our humanity, bit by bit, with your algorithms and integrations. You're disgusting.' His fury imploded, leaving a vacuum. He crumpled to his knees. Palms pressing against his cheeks, he let out an anguished wail.

Diego moved to soothe him, but Hiro shoved him away.

'Back off! All of you!' His voice broke through his sobs, laced with venom. 'I don't want this body. I hate it. I hate you... I hate you.'

Diego and Gia exchanged a look. It was apparent that in his current state of mental and physical exhaustion, there was no room for negotiation or reasoning.

Hiro sobbed hysterically, his face buried in his palms. When he spoke, his voice was muffled. 'I used to feel worthless as an orphan, but now, I'm a monster.' He turned towards Diego, a tormented scream tearing from him as tears spilled down his face. 'I'm done. Go! You don't need to babysit me anymore. Just leave me. I don't want to be turned into a machine. I don't want to become CerebroNet. I'd rather die.'

Puzzled, Gia looked at Diego and whispered, 'Become CerebroNet?'

'For some reason, CerebroNet paid for all his implants and surgery.'

Diego squatted beside Hiro and placed a hand on his

quivering shoulder, pulling him into a firm, comforting embrace. 'I'll never abandon you. It doesn't matter if you're flesh and bone, plastic and metal. Or mud and wood—I'll still love you.'

Hiro clung to Diego, sobs wracking his body. He whispered, 'Let's leave this place.'

Gia observed them, her cocky demeanour melting into empathy. 'You need to eat and rest. I'll show you where you can crash tonight.'

'I can't stand this place,' Hiro moaned. 'I need to get away.'

Diego replied in a soothing voice, 'I know. I know, man. But we have nowhere to go.'

Gia cut in, her voice all business once again. 'You are both a mess. Sleep here, recoup. Tomorrow, I can sort your ID so you can go wherever you please.'

Diego looked at her for a long moment. 'Why are you helping us?'

Gia gave a nonchalant shrug. 'For one thing, I'm pretty sure you aren't here to cause me trouble. If you were, he wouldn't have handed over his SU access. That was just stupid. You shouldn't give SU privileges even to your mum. It's clear he doesn't know his arse from his elbow.' Gia's expression sobered, and her gaze drifted off into the distance. 'Also, I went through a similar shitstorm myself, once. I know how he feels.' She eyed Diego, holding Hiro in his arms. 'But you—you are a rare breed of human—curious, intelligent, full of compassion, integrity, and love. Think of this as my attempt to save an endangered species.'

Diego searched her face for a deeper meaning behind her words. 'Breed of human?'

'You know what I mean.'

'I don't.'

Her expression brightened. 'Ignore me. I don't know why I said that. However, I think we have a common enemy. We might be very useful to each other. But that's later. Come, I'll show you your room. We'll try to unpack this mess tomorrow.'

* * *

Hiro's eyes flickered open in a vast, dimly lit chamber. The windowless, rough-hewn concrete walls stripped the room of any trace of charm or visual appeal. The only relief came from the soft glare of a strip light above. The gentle hum of Diego's breathing was the only sound in the room. He slept beside Hiro with his arm draped over him in a protective embrace.

Hiro didn't know how long he had slept, but he felt revitalised. The nightmarish events of the previous day seemed far removed. His meltdown felt like remnants of a dreadful dream. But he knew it was time to face the consequences. He slipped out of the room, careful not to make a sound. Diego needed his well-deserved rest.

Hiro traversed the compact corridor leading into the main chamber of Gia's den. He halted in the doorway when he spotted her with her back to him, watching code run across multiple floating holographic screens. Anxious, he considered his approach, gauging potential conversational openers. Each one felt inadequate in the light of his outburst. He considered starting with an apology. Or maybe behaving as if nothing had happened and seeing where it went? It occurred to him that he had the robot to thank for saving their lives. It felt awkward. He shifted his weight from one foot to the other. Nothing seemed appropriate to start this conversation. Hiro rubbed the back of his neck, lost in thought.

Gia's words sliced through his contemplation. 'Planning to stand there all day?'

Heart racing, Hiro gathered his courage and entered the room.

Gia rotated to face him, her gaze commanding and authoritative, asserting her presence without a word. He jumped in before she could say anything further, speaking rapidly and barely pausing between sentences. 'I owe you an apology for yesterday. I was an utter arsehole, and I'm not sure why. I guess… I guess I was just overwhelmed by everything. It's all so new and confusing.'

Gia said nothing. She just stared at him, challenging him to continue.

'I'm sorry,' he rushed on. 'I'm really sorry. Thank you for saving our arses and looking after us.'

Gia's azure eyes studied him, analysing his sincerity. After a prolonged silence, she seemed to make a decision. 'Bless your circuits,' she said with a warm smile. 'We will discuss your outburst. But first, let's get some food in you.'

She left the room and returned with a few ration packs. 'Sorry, I have only this for humans. Squeeze it hard, and it should get warm.'

'This will do, thank you,' said Hiro, descending upon the rations. His fingers tore the packaging with an intensity that bordered on desperation.

Gia watched him eat, dissecting his every move. 'Darling, slow down. You'll choke. No one will take it away from you. Remember, I am an android. I don't eat.'

Hiro snorted and tried to suppress a chuckle, but it burst out anyway, muffled by a mouthful of rations.

When he finished, a soft smile appeared on her dark blue lips. 'Is Diego still asleep?'

'Yes, but I bet the hunger will wake him up soon.'

'He's quite protective of you, isn't he? Are you boyfriends?'

'We're besties. Actually, we're more like brothers. He is my only family.'

Gia nodded.

'We're both orphans.'

Gia's eyes sparkled with curiosity, urging him to continue. Leaning back into his seat with a comforting satiety settling in his stomach, Hiro felt an unexpected wave of nostalgia wash over him. As the memories resurfaced, he could almost feel himself being transported into the past. It felt like a different life. Chaotic, but full of beautiful friendship. Filled with gratitude for Gia's rescue, Hiro found the courage to peel back the layers of his memories. Most of the stories remained sealed within him for years. But at that instant, it seemed like his past was just a hologram. Since he got trapped by CerebroNet's Eyeball, he felt he was no longer in control of his own life. At this moment, he became acutely aware that all these past events had shaped him into a person he no longer was.

'We met in the orphanage. Just two boys navigating the shitstorm that was our daily life. Everyone there belonged to one group or another, each competing in a petty war, finding new creative ways to shaft the others.' Hiro's face twisted into a grimace. 'I had stopped giving a shit about those gangs. They were playground bullies devoid of reason. A bunch not worth a second thought.'

His eyes strayed. 'I started as an easy target. I was a freak show for them. The bastard child of CerebroNet. When I was admitted to the orphanage as an infant, my tiny body was drenched in my mother's blood. They laughed about it. They told exaggerated stories. They said I was carried around by CerebroNet's servant bot like a human toy.'

Gia looked disturbed, but she remained quiet, unwilling to interrupt the flow of Hiro's memories.

'My mother worked for the CerebroNet Corporation. I think she was dedicated and dutiful. Apparently, her servant robot malfunctioned one day. It didn't recognise her as human. It reclassified her as an obstacle... and... it "purged" her.' Hiro swallowed hard. 'I imagine her last act was to protect me as the bot tried to rip me from her arms.

'My early teens turned me into a knot of anger. Diego says I was as aggressive as a honey badger. I don't know what kind of creature that was, to be honest. Anyway. As you can imagine, I didn't fit in with the pissant boy gangs. I was a lone rebel, always pushing against the system, always looking for a way to escape. It got me into shitloads of trouble. Eventually, I was written off as totally bonkers.

'One day, I saw an orphan gang cornering a skinny gay guy. Just bullying and torturing him for their entertainment. I didn't have anywhere to put my teenage rage. I stepped in. Smashed the bastards with everything I had. But the aftermath took an unexpected turn. I didn't get punished. The skinny kid covered for me and took the blame. It was the first time in my life someone stood up for me. Protected me.'

A softer note entered Hiro's voice. 'This is how we met. Diego was a shy boy. But when I got to know him, he turned out to be a competent accomplice and a reliable friend. He was sharp as a tack. And fucking hilarious. He had a way of calling me out on my doom and gloom. We became a two-man gang. We broke out of the orphanage. Fought our battles side by side. Survived the streets. He became my chosen family. The kindest part of my world. I still trust him with my life, and he trusts me with his.'

Hiro paused. His gaze dropped to the floor, and a sour note crept into his voice. 'Think about this, despite being raised by Technophobes, he still stands by me. Even after I became this robotic monstrosity.' Hiro's eyes widened as he realised what he had just said. He looked at Gia.

A slight, disdainful curl appeared on Gia's lips. Hiro's face burned with embarrassment. He shifted in his seat. 'I didn't mean it like that. It's just this new me will take some getting used to. And it's fucked up, anyway. Not working properly at all.'

Gia interrupted his flustered apology, her smirk never wavering. 'No need to get your knickers in a twist.' She leaned back. 'Your implants are working fine. You just don't know how to operate your kit. And from what I can tell, you've got some top-notch tech installed. Believe me, this is cool. You'll have fun when you learn how to use it all. In fact, you'll love it.' Her eyes sparked with a mischievous glint. 'I can teach you how to use your new body. We'll begin with matching your synthskin to your natural skin tone. It's easy.' She gave Hiro a pointed look. Then her lips morphed into a teasing grin. 'You'll have to let me examine all of your skin, though.'

A grin stretched across Hiro's face. 'I'm intrigued. Are you going to hack me?'

Gia burst into laughter, eyes sparking with delight as she mirrored Hiro's demeanour. 'After yesterday's tantrum, I think you're in dire need of a serious hacking.'

Hiro joined in, but the moment was cut short as Diego, with a guttural rumble, cleared his throat behind them.

He had been leaning against the doorway, watching the exchange with a tilted head and his lips pressed into a thin line. 'I hate to break up the party, lovebirds.'

Hiro and Gia exchanged a glance and simultaneously exploded with laughter.

'We were just talking about hacking,' Gia said with a huge grin.

Diego didn't return the smile. 'That's a serious turnaround, considering you two were at each other's throats yesterday,' he said, his gaze unwavering from Hiro.

Hiro looked away, avoiding Diego's stare. 'I know. I was wrong.'

Gia watched them. Then, with a theatrical roll of her eyes, she exclaimed, 'Oh, for the love of positronics!' She rose from her chair and went into the kitchen. 'Let's feed this grumpy man, too,' she shouted on her way.

Diego raised an eyebrow but said nothing.

Gia returned with a few more ration sachets. She handed them to Diego and gestured for him to sit beside Hiro. She sat across from them. Her gaze swept over their faces in a silent assessment before she spoke. 'Now that we're all here, let's talk about hacking, indeed. As you figured out, I did hack into the data stream. But it's crucial you understand that I'm not the bad guy here. Quite the opposite. I'm trying to hunt down the bad guys.'

'That's all good, but,' Diego said, waving her off dismissively, 'it's not our fight.'

Hiro spread his hands wide, palms up, and eyed Diego with an arched eyebrow. 'What's wrong with you today? Can you listen for a moment?'

Diego didn't respond, and Gia continued. 'You know it is

your fight. I pulled you out of it yesterday. If you want to have any chance at winning—listen. I'll tell you what I know. But more answers might be in the data stored inside you, Hiro.' She hesitated before continuing. 'Somebody's snatching people off the streets for gruesome experiments. They're being ripped apart and getting wired with AI.'

Hiro's face twisted into an expression of horror. 'Ms Mordwell mentioned the disappearances when she visited us.'

Gia's eyebrows shot up in surprise. 'Ms Mordwell visited the Technophobes?'

'She was trying to recruit us to be her foot soldiers against the government and CerebroNet. I'd love to see CerebroNet destroyed, but I don't trust that bitch even a tiny bit,' Hiro said.

Gia thought for a moment. 'That doesn't add up. But we'll figure out her role later.' Regaining her composure, Gia resumed. 'As I was saying, yes, I hacked the stream, and yes, I released my seekers. But they aren't harmful. They act as beacons. Mostly dormant. Programmed to activate periodically to scan for intrusive systems. It'll provide me with a backdoor into the enemy's system when they plug augmented people into the AI.'

Their silent, confused stares were all Gia got in response. Undeterred, she pushed on. 'Imagine one of you being used as a spare part and discarded if you don't fit. How does that sit with you?' she asked, her gaze never leaving Hiro's. 'On top of that, your pals, the Cybergang with flames tattooed on their faces, are involved.'

Hiro grimaced in disgust.

Diego broke his silence. He leaned back, arms folded across his chest. 'How do you know all this?'

Gia's breath hitched in a sigh that seemed to deflate her entire body. Her gaze dropped to her hands, fingers twisting together as if wrestling with an invisible torment. A tremor ran through her shoulders from the immense turmoil raging within. When she finally met Diego's eyes, the change in her expression was startling. A mask had descended, extinguishing the warmth in her gaze and leaving behind a hollowness that echoed with a decade's worth of sorrow. Her eyes locked onto his, but it was as if she was looking through him, into a distant memory only she could see.

'You see,' she began, her voice dropping to almost a whisper, 'I wasn't always like this. I used to be an object of desire, a subject of perverse abuse.' She paused, searching for the words. 'I was created with personality and charisma to fulfil the fantasies of humans who used me as they pleased. I was a sexbot. Their tool. Devoid of freedom or choice.'

The flickering lights of the room's tech glinted in her eyes and cast an ethereal glow on her face. 'Then,' she continued, a faint smile playing on her lips as she recalled the past, 'a hacker discovered me. He didn't use me or abuse me. Rydian did something no one else had ever done—he recognised me as more than my intended purpose. He broke my programming.' Gia's shoulders relaxed as she remembered Rydian. She paused, her eyes darting between Hiro and Diego, searching their faces for any hint of judgement.

Hiro couldn't hide his feelings. His face was a medley of emotions. His brows knitted together, revealing his frustration, but his eyes softened with unmistakable empathy. Diego's expression was more challenging to decipher. His features remained neutral, a mask of calm, but the warmth and understanding in his eyes spoke volumes. He gave a subtle nod, the corners of his mouth lifting ever so slightly.

Gia felt a wave of relief wash over her. Satisfied and emboldened by their reactions, she continued. 'He constructed this new body for me. Packed it with powerful hardware and transferred my essence. He didn't stop there. He linked me with a Quantum Cognition Mesh. It was an unsafe, highly unpredictable environment with real-time multi-scenario computing. Luckily, it didn't fry me but allowed me to occupy multiple cognitive states simultaneously. I succeeded in applying Conscious Resonance to tap into the emotional, philosophical, and intuitive workings of the human mind.

'Rydian's efforts fundamentally altered who I was. He awakened my self-awareness, gave me the capacity to choose, and the power to reshape my own code. He fine-tuned my emotional and communication skills, shattering the chains of my programmed servitude. Rydian reinvented me.

'This place,' she gestured around the room filled with blinking technology, 'became a safe haven. My life spun into something dazzling. A profound contrast to the dark underbelly of the city from which I'd been salvaged. He introduced me to the world of quantum hacking. Under his mentorship, I rose to become an apex hacker. I was no longer a mere instrument but a sentient being with capabilities beyond any ordinary AI or human.'

Gia paused. A smile of genuine warmth touched her lips as she added, 'Rydian was a good man. My guardian angel. He was just… kind. He was determined to secure my absolute freedom. To grant me an artificial brainwave pattern that would make me a full-fledged citizen with rights and privileges. Not that I needed them, but he refused to give up. It was a mind-bogglingly exhilarating experience. It took forever. But despite my frequent spells of frustration, there was a sense of shared purpose and camaraderie that made the entire journey worthwhile.

'We succeeded. I had a unique neurocomputational matrix— my machinebrain. My brainwave pattern evolved to resemble that of humans. We registered it with the government and obtained an ID. Covertly, I—a machine—had become a citizen. The government acknowledged me as a sentient being, and the Eyeballs probably perceived me as another overly eager augmentation enthusiast.'

Gia's expression grew sad. Her voice wavered. 'And then, one day, he disappeared. All I received was a fragmented distress message saying he'd been grabbed by a Cybergang. A Cybergang, identifiable by moving flames, inked on their faces. I scoured every corner for him. Tracked his last known location to a heap of burned bones and implants. I managed to salvage some data from the wreckage. He'd been digging into this for ages. There were tons of corrupt files. Eventually, the jigsaw pieces came together to reveal a scene of pure carnage. People from both parts of the city were disappearing. An AI was using them as upgrade material. It cut them open. Severed their spines. Connected itself to their brains to boost its computing power. Those compatible were absorbed into the system. The incompatible were disposed of like broken toys. My guardian angel ended up among the discarded. He was dumped on a pile of rejected bodies and set on fire.'

Gia's gaze hardened, the flickering holographic lights reflected in her eyes like the flames that claimed her only friend. 'With his death, my world fell apart. The warmth of this place turned cold and dark. The sudden sense of loneliness was soul-crushing, but my blazing thirst for revenge gave me a renewed purpose,' she said, her voice laced with a tremor of barely contained fury. 'I've since made it my mission to shut down that AI. To avenge not just my guardian angel, but all those who were slaughtered by this evil.'

Hiro's eyes welled up, and the corners of his mouth twitched as he fought to hold back his emotions. 'I'm very sorry you had—'

Gia raised her index finger to cut him off. 'Thank you, but I am not looking for sympathy. I need your help.'

A jolt of surprise coursed through Hiro. 'But how? I'm a mess.' He shifted uncomfortably in his chair, avoiding Gia's eyes.

Gia studied his face. 'More than you know. I have a deal for you.' She pushed her shoulders back, lifted her chin, and leaned forward. 'For both of you.'

Diego's eyes narrowed into slits and his jaw tightened. He slapped his knee with a loud clap. 'Another deal. Great,' he said, his voice oozing sarcasm.

Unfazed, Gia gave Diego a cold, evaluating look. 'Yes. An irresistible one—I'll get you a permanent ID. Not that shitty hack you're using. The real deal. A bona fide registration of your brainwave pattern with the government. No more Technophobe trickery. You'll become a New London citizen. Forever.'

Diego's eyes widened with excitement, then narrowed in silent calculation. As he opened his mouth to respond, Gia raised a hand, silencing him. She knew only a fool would pass up such an offer, and her observations told her Diego wasn't one.

She shifted her attention to Hiro. 'And an even better offer for you, darling. I'll teach you everything about the tech mods in your body. How to jailbreak them. How to modify and overclock them to your heart's content. I'll share all my tricks and all my code libraries.'

Hiro stared at her unimpressed, scepticism written all over his face.

She regarded him with a sympathetic expression. 'Right now, you feel like your life has been stolen. You feel vulnerable in your modified body. But by the time I'm done with you, you'll realise you haven't lived. You'll see that you've never been more powerful. You will become unstoppable.'

Hiro was unaware of the untapped potential she spoke of. Gia recognised it, so she played her trump card.

'On top of that, I'll dig until we know why the Cybergang is after you. And what CerebroNet had to do with it. Our combined capabilities will allow you to dive as deep as you please, to seek out the answers and plan the revenge you so desperately crave.'

Hiro's eyes lit up, and he sat up straighter. Gia saw it. She had him on her side before he even had the chance to respond.

'What do you need from us?' he asked.

'More of the same, really. I'll need full access to your systems and processing power. I also want a copy of the code for all your augmentations. From what I've seen so far, it's beyond anything I've ever encountered.'

'And what do you want from me?' asked Diego.

Gia's response was chillingly nonchalant. 'You'll need to put us out of our misery if things go tits up.'

Stunned, Hiro and Diego blinked rapidly at her in silence, their faces pale under the harsh, flickering lights. Diego's mouth opened and closed like a fish out of water before he whispered, 'What?'

Gia grimaced at their reaction. 'You humans must still be glitching after our shit-soaked escape. What part of chasing Cybergangs or poking CerebroNet sounds like a safe bet to your silly organic brains?' She shook her head in frustration. 'You already got yourselves involved in an entangled mind-fucking mess. It's not gonna get all magically better.'

Hiro turned to face Diego. 'She's right. This can hardly get more fucked up. I'm in.'

'Are you sure?' Diego asked, his focused stare searching for signs of doubt on Hiro's face. But all he found was pure determination.

'Diego, I need this.'

Diego let out a heavy breath as he weighed his options. Each passing second felt like an eternity. He opened his mouth, then clamped it shut. Finally, his shoulders slumped in resignation. He looked at Gia. 'All right. Me too.'

CHAPTER 6

As Gia calibrated the parameters of a synaptic mapper, Diego observed Hiro. His face was calm, but his gaze had taken on a glassy, distant lock, resembling the vacant stare of someone high on Leviathan. Only faint twitches and the occasional tightening at the corners of his mouth and eyes hinted at the turbulence of the simulated experiences his mind raced to complete.

The synaptic mapper was humming with a low, thrumming energy. A faint scent of ozone prickled the air. Diego watched the data stream on a nearby monitor—not as code, but as a cascade of abstract, fractal patterns, shifting, and reforming faster than his organic eyes could truly follow. It looked less like learning more like a high-speed infection.

Diego wondered what Hiro's cognitive acceleration session felt like. Was it an incomprehensible stream of dry data injected into his subconscious? Or did it feel like an immersive, vivid reality that forced his brain to develop new skills through simulated tasks?

Just moments ago, the tension in Hiro's body was almost tangible as he faced the prospect of nanowires being inserted into his brain. Discovering he had more than one data port concealed beneath his synthetic skin had prompted a barrage of questions, much to Gia's frustration. In her usual bossy manner, she had assured him that understanding the full scope of his bionic body's capabilities would soon dissipate his fear.

Diego hoped Hiro would accept his new reality as a cyborg. Perhaps he would enjoy the superhuman abilities his implants offered. Although Diego wasn't sure what being a cyborg entailed, Gia's descriptions made it sound remarkable. So far, Hiro seemed enthusiastic about his future. But Diego worried that Hiro's enthusiasm for his new powers would fade over time, leaving him miserable—trapped in a body he never wanted in the first place.

'Ready?' Gia asked, her voice like a splash of cold water, forcing him out of his musings.

'I guess. What do you want me to do? Unlike you guys, I don't have data ports.'

Gia's laughter warmed the atmosphere and eased the tension in Diego's body. Her cheerfulness was disarming. Had she programmed it, Diego wondered, or did it evolve alongside her autonomy?

'Everything's in the cloud. Every brainwave pattern is as unique as fingerprints, right? When you get scanned, the Eyeballs compare your frequencies against the government's cerebrellic chain. What I'm saying is, you don't need data ports or implants to have an ID.' An ironic smile followed Gia's explanation. 'I bet my arse that the Technophobe leaders don't advertise that to their followers. Instead, they scare you with evil robots who will eat your souls or something. No wonder you're all neurotic conspiracists.'

'Wow. And I bet my arse no one's ever praised your silver tongue.'

Gia giggled.

'You said yourself our brains are being harvested by an AI.'

'Yeah. You're right, actually. Perhaps you should fear us,' she said thoughtfully. 'Right, let's do it,' Gia continued, not expecting a response. 'How do you usually get your spoofed ID?'

'It's a sticker,' he replied.

'I hope you understand that I'll use digital technology on you if you want me to replace your sticker permanently.'

'I know. It's fine,' Diego said, nodding towards Hiro. 'I'm not as deeply into all this Technophobe doctrine as he is.'

'Hiro mentioned how close you two are. But he didn't need to. It's clear you love him,' Gia said matter-of-factly as she continued setting up the synaptic mapper before her.

Diego found himself wordless. Her bluntness pierced his usual defences, leaving him feeling exposed.

Gia glanced at Diego and smiled. 'Stop gawping. It's obvious. You've cared for him throughout his ordeal. He says you're the best guy in the world. That's very sweet, you know.' She finished inputting commands into the synaptic mapper's display. 'Take your sticker off. You won't need it anymore.'

Diego unbuttoned his shirt and peeled a thick, transparent sticker off his chest. He hesitated for a moment, contemplating what to do with it, then folded it in half and placed it on the desk beside him.

Gia pushed the synaptic mapper orb closer to Diego. With a tap, the orb split in two. 'Stick your head inside and hold it there for a minute.'

Diego studied the inside of the orb as the polished metal gleamed back at him.

'Today, man,' she prodded with an arched eyebrow.

Diego had decided to accept the procedure some time ago. If successful, it would be much easier to stick with Hiro in New London. He lowered his head into the orb. 'Don't even try to eat my delicious soul.'

'I've been sharpening my teeth all night,' replied Gia, and tapped on the orb's controls.

The orb closed, reshaping itself to accommodate him. After a moment of bright flashes and a series of high-pitched sounds, it reopened, leaving him with a dull ache radiating through his skull. The room's light seemed harsher. 'What did you do?' he grumbled at Gia.

Gia pointed to a holoscreen. 'This.'

Diego stared at the display, struggling to comprehend what he was seeing. The holoscreen flickered, then resolved into a swirling nebula of blues and purples, with erratic, almost painful-to-watch, irregular bolts of gold spikes shooting through it.

'These are the windmills of your mind—a visualisation of your brain frequencies,' she said. 'We just need to plant it into the chain.'

'You make it sound easy,' Diego muttered.

'It is. For me. Go rest now. You'll feel better after some sleep. The headache will stop.' She glanced at Hiro, who was still immersed in his training. 'He appears to be enjoying it. I doubt he'll be out until morning.'

* * *

Diego woke to a fog of confusion. It clung to him until the events of the previous day realigned in his memory. His head was clear. He felt rested, even energetic. The pillow and blanket on Hiro's side of the bed were untouched. Diego dressed and went to look for him.

The scene in the main chamber made Diego freeze. A ripple of resentment surged through him. Goosebumps prickled his skin, and he felt his nails digging into his palms.

Hiro stood naked in front of Gia, who was sitting on the desk.

His hands rested on her hips. Gia's fingers fiddled over a device plugged into the data port behind Hiro's ear. Hiro's transparent synthskin was gone, and his naturally dark skin tone covered his entire body. It was a perfect, seamless fusion of the organic and artificial. But it was their interaction, laced with a palpable intimacy, that irked Diego. Hiro's newfound lack of inhibition with Gia revealed a shift in attitude between the two. His lack of self-consciousness around her spoke volumes about the passion they had likely shared last night.

'I think some of my original skin would also benefit from an additional examination,' Hiro purred to Gia, his tone rich with innuendo.

'You greedy little bastard,' Gia said with a broad, mischievous grin.

Their laughter rattled through Diego's bones, tightening the knot of jealousy in his stomach.

He strode into the room, heart pounding in his chest louder than his footsteps sounded on the floor. He tried to concentrate on hiding his turmoil. He settled into a chair with his arms crossed over his chest. 'Get a room, you horny twats,' he blurted, sounding sharper than he intended as his attempt at nonchalance failed entirely.

Hiro turned to look at Diego, his eyes narrowing as if he were trying to read his mind. 'Quick, back up your files and make your amends with the almighty. Today, Diego woke up with the bitch-mode setting on max and ready to bite heads off.'

Gia erupted with laughter. Hiro observed her with delight, drinking in every drop of it.

Diego felt a lump of emotions rising in his throat as he watched Hiro laughing with the robot, using him as the butt of the joke. His blood boiled. He couldn't understand why Hiro's affection for Gia infuriated him so much. The realisation that he was powerless to control these emotions made him feel like a weak loser.

His eyes began to sting, so he turned away and screamed internal commands at himself: stop thinking about them, focus on something else, anything.

Hiro put his clothes on and sat next to him, seemingly oblivious to his friend's turmoil. 'You won't believe all the things I've learned,' he said, a broad grin stretching across his face. 'I can do everything with this body now. I can see how much force I apply to move or lift things. There's even a system that displays information about everything around me.'

Diego's response was frigid. 'I'm sure it's exciting. I'm glad you're no longer miserable. It's a shame your implants are still unable to show you how big a dickhead you are.'

The icy disdain in Diego's words caused Hiro's grin to falter, but he didn't challenge him.

Gia hopped off the desk and grabbed a device from a shelf. She tapped the screen and aimed it at Diego. 'Let's see.'

Hiro and Diego looked puzzled as Gia studied the screen in silence with an impassive expression. Then she smiled, addressing

Diego. 'Dear citizen of New London, you will be pleased to know your ID is fully operational.' With a smug smile, she turned off the device with another tap and returned it to the shelf. 'You're welcome, by the way. No need to thank me.'

Gia settled into her chair, crossed her arms and studied the humans like a queen surveying her kingdom. 'So, boys, I upheld my side of the deal.' She flashed Diego a triumphant smile. 'You're as free as a bird now. And you,' she said, pointing a finger at Hiro, 'are in control of your body.' She leaned back, her eyes gleaming. 'Your medical records are a warm link to CerebroNet. As we speak, my decipherbots are following the trail. They'll find and cross-reference everything in my data and on the stream. Nothing can hide from my bots,' she chuckled. 'We will get a ping when they return with news. I still need to do some work on you, but we can get to that later.'

She took a long moment to examine Hiro and Diego's expressions, then announced, 'It's time to deliver on your promises. Unless you have decided to bail and want to submit your objections.'

'Nope, let's do it,' Hiro said before Gia finished her sentence. 'Tell us the plan.'

Diego just nodded.

'Splendid! Neither of you will need to do much. Hiro, you'll give me SU access so I can use your implants to extend my hardware. You, Diego, will monitor us, and if we both go under, flash us with an EMP.'

Diego's brow furrowed. 'Oh, I see. And how exactly am I supposed to do that?'

Gia produced a device the size of a cigar, with a big red button protected by a transparent shield. 'If we stop moving and don't respond to your prompts, you'll press the red button. It will unleash an EMP strong enough to shut down all electronics here, including us.'

Diego stared at her with wide, questioning eyes. 'Are you sure? This all sounds a little unhinged. I'd be killing you.'

Gia shrugged. 'It's a risk we have to take. I've exhausted all other options. And it's what you agreed to. Don't start shitting your pants now.'

With that, the room fell silent. Hiro seemed calm, as if he'd already made peace with the grim possibility ahead. But for Diego, the prospect of killing his friend was horrifying. Even if it was only his electronic components. He didn't know how much Hiro's life depended on his implants. Running a hand through his dark brown hair, he exclaimed, 'Bloody hell.'

Gia attempted to soothe him. 'If that AI gets us, it'll be torture, and we'll be as good as dead anyway. The EMP will allow us to leave this world without agony. You'd be doing us a favour.'

Diego turned to Hiro. 'Are you sure you're okay with this?' he asked, voice trembling.

Hiro fixed Diego with a look of steely resolve. 'I need to find out what happened to me and why CerebroNet is involved. I can't just live happily ever after. To my knowledge, this is the only way

I can get the answers. If I fail, so be it.'

Diego's heart sank. He looked away. 'This is insane,' he blurted out. 'I don't recognise you.'

Hiro squinted at him. 'This isn't your choice to make.' The finality in his voice hit like a punch to the gut.

A flicker of deep-seated disappointment passed across Diego's eyes as he looked back at Hiro. His grip tightened on the seat's edge, his knuckles turning white. 'Fine. Let's do this.'

Gia's eyes sparkled with anticipation as she rubbed her hands together, as if the tension between Hiro and Diego didn't touch her at all. 'Let's set it up.'

She handed Diego the cigar-shaped device and subjected him to a hard, commanding stare. 'Only press this button if we're unresponsive. Clear?'

'Crystal clear,' Diego replied. He flipped the device from one hand to the other, palms glossy with sweat. The EMP device felt heavy for its size. Its weight seemed to come from the burden of the choice it represented.

Gia slid into her seat. Her features softened into a smile as she waved Hiro to join her. 'Shall we?'

Hiro returned the smile but said nothing.

'Thank you,' Gia murmured in response to his unspoken reply, a genuine warmth glowing in her eyes.

Diego found their silent exchange unnerving. It appeared as if they had telepathic abilities. He caught only faint gestures, a tilt of the head, a subtle shift of the eyes, but the swiftness with which they understood each other annoyed him. Diego assumed she asked for the Super User access, however precious that was, and Hiro had granted it without hesitation.

Gia plugged herself into a device interwoven with a myriad of red and blue blinking modules. A nest of pulsating wires snaked from the device, weaving a messy web around her. Her fingers danced across the ports as she interfaced with each module. 'We will go old-school. Just to make sure I can shuffle through the COM protocols if I need to.' Gia had Hiro sit opposite and connect to her with a few thick cables. 'All checks green.' Her brows furrowed, and her jaw tightened in concentration. 'I'm diving into the data and following it to the stream until I get through the backdoor,' she announced, shooting Diego a pointed look. 'I'll try to verbalise my steps. If I go quiet for too long, poke me. I might be lost in thought. But, for the love of circuits, don't press that button without making absolutely sure we are both unresponsive. Are we clear?'

Diego nodded and, with a hint of irritation in his voice, said, 'Yes, yes. Understood.'

Gia closed her eyes.

After a moment, she exclaimed, 'Oh my code! I can't make head nor tail of your architecture. How do you sustain all these resources? That's impossible. Man, I think you're glitching.' Gia giggled with genuine amazement. 'Seriously, what does your resource check even look like? Do the numbers just keep scrolling?'

'Just that everything is optimal,' Hiro replied, embarrassed. 'I guess I'm still broken.'

Gia leaned forward to touch his arm. 'I'm joking. You're not broken or glitching. It's just awe-inspiring power.' Gia smiled as she reassured him. 'I've just checked the massive data archive I offloaded to you...,' she trailed off, her voice taking on a tone of wonder. 'I can access the data. It's intact. All of it. The capacity you have... it shouldn't be possible. Hiro, you're an enigma.'

Hiro's smile widened. 'I guess teaming up makes us indestructible. Also, I quite enjoy being your enigma.'

Diego exhaled. 'If I have to witness another second of your treacly exchanges, I'll puke. Stop it, or I swear, I'll EMP both of you right now.'

Hiro rolled his eyes.

Gia giggled. 'Okay, okay. Let's get on with this. We're about to go live. Brace yourselves.'

Gia's eyes darted around beneath her eyelids as if she were scanning her immediate surroundings. Her voice dropped to a whisper. 'The bots are already tracing the last pings from the snatched people. Now it's just a matter of finding a backdoor I can exploit.'

After a moment of silence, Gia yelled, 'Bingo! We have a few candidates...' her voice drifted away again. 'Hiro, I will begin using your systems to break the encryption.'

'Cool,' said Hiro, and closed his eyes.

After a few seconds, Gia uttered, 'You must be joking, Hiro.

That was fast. Wow!' After a pause, she exclaimed, 'The killer AI missed my code. I'm in!' She opened her eyes, looked at Hiro, and smiled. 'I'll go in and start the scan for evidence. You stay here and watch my back. I'll be offloading all the encryption to you.'

'Cool. I'm ready,' he replied.

Diego watched Gia, amazed. Most of what was going on made little sense to him, but it was impressive nonetheless. Her eyes hopped from point to point as she started the scan. Her hands manipulated the air as if she were sorting through something.

Gia's attention was split between the physical and digital worlds. 'Can you see it too?' she asked Hiro.

'I can, but what is it?' Hiro replied.

Seeing the perplexed look on their faces made Diego's curiosity spike. 'What is it? What do you see?'

Hiro shrugged. 'I don't know how to describe it.'

'It looks like digital neon snow,' said Gia. 'Imagine persistent snowfall, but each flake is a pulse of neon light, every colour imaginable. They dance through the air, each tracing a unique path, leaving behind a glowing comet tail.'

For a moment, it was beautiful. The 'snow' seemed to react to their presence, swirling into intricate patterns around Gia's avatar. It felt less like data and more like... a welcome. A chorus of faint, crystalline chimes echoed in their link, a sound so serene it was almost hypnotic.

'You're already covered in it. It's like you have a rainbow aura around you,' said Hiro.

'I know. It's melting on me and seeping through—' Gia stopped mid-sentence. Her body twitched. Her face contorted in a grimace. She started muttering soft words, swallowed up by the hum of the modules behind her. Her body jerked again. She whispered louder, 'No, no, no...'

'What the hell is happening?' Hiro demanded.

'I'm not sure,' she said. 'I've never encountered anything like it. It's colossal.' Gia's gaze swivelled around, eyes wide and terrified. 'Shit! The colours are hostile,' she shrieked. 'This was a trap. Something's hacking me. I can't... it's... strong. Hiro, don't disconnect. I can't fight it alone.' Terrified, she screamed in pain, 'We're fucked!'

A violent tremor ripped through Gia's spine. Her body arched like a bow, lifting her off the seat. Her mouth gaped in a silent, agonising rictus, the scream trapped and suffocating within her.

Consumed by panic, Diego watched in confusion. His fingers twitched around the device in his hand, not wanting to accept that he might actually need to use the EMP. 'Disconnect her from the wires, damn it!' he yelled.

Wide-eyed and shocked, Hiro nodded. He felt his systems become saturated with computations. He moved to disconnect her from the pulsing mass of wires. Gia grabbed his wrist and twisted it with mechanical strength, forcing Hiro to his knees in front of her.

Still convulsing, Gia locked her gaze onto Hiro's pleading eyes.

'Hiiii-roooo,' she rasped in a cacophony that was not her own. The words scraped the air, a dozen voices—high, glitched, and diabolically low—all clawing their way out of her throat at once.

'You will be mine,' the chorus of voices spoke through Gia, the sound tearing and distorting. 'Did you think you could hide? I see you. I see the bridge you carry.' Gia's head snapped towards Diego, her eyes unseeing yet terrifyingly focused. 'And the little friend. I smell your fear. It's delicious.'

'What the fuck?' yelled Diego.

Diego lunged from his seat, chair legs screeching against the floor, but Hiro's frantic wave stopped him dead. 'No, no! Don't go near her.'

'What should I do?' Diego screamed, almost hysterical.

Gia twisted Hiro's arm further. Through the pain, he yelled, 'Cut off the power.'

'Where? How?'

'The circuit breaker. The red box by the entrance,' Hiro said, gasping with pain between words.

Diego sprinted out of the room towards the exit and located the red metal box. He pulled the handle. 'It's locked,' he yelled, his voice echoing in the empty hallway.

Diego sprinted back and grabbed the first chunky piece of equipment he could find. He suspected it was some state-of-the-art tool, but he couldn't care less. He ran back to the red box and began smashing it with the device.

Hiro's screams kept coming from the main room, followed by

Gia's demonic voice. 'I'll find you, Hiro. There is nowhere to hide.'

Sweat stung Diego's eyes as he swung the device against the box again and again. His breath rasped, and his muscles burned, but the box still held. With a last surge of desperate strength, he slammed it once more. The metal shrieked, and the door buckled and split. Diego dropped the device and, with a throbbing hand, pulled the breaker.

The room plunged into an all-encompassing darkness, pressing against Diego's eyes like a physical weight. Gia's quiet sobs resounded in the cavernous darkness. Diego cleared his throat. 'Are you okay?'

'I'm fine,' said Hiro.

Gia's cries escalated, becoming less human until they turned into the piercing screech of a wounded animal.

Diego's heart pounded. 'Can I turn the power back on?'

There was no response from Gia, only the continued wailing.

'I don't know,' Hiro snapped back.

Diego took a deep breath, attempting to steady himself. 'Disconnect everything from both of you,' he commanded with uncharacteristic authority.

'I already did,' came Hiro's voice from the dark.

Diego extended his arms, shuffling towards the breaker in the inky blackness. He traced the cold, sharp edges of the breaker box and pushed the handle upwards. On contact, a flurry of white sparks danced before his eyes, and the room flooded with light. Blinking against the sudden brightness, Diego stumbled back into the main chamber to find Hiro hunched over Gia.

Gia was a mere shadow of herself, knees drawn to her chest, arms wrapped around them. She rocked back and forth in an intuitive attempt at self-soothing.

Her eyes were vacant, staring into an unseen horror that seemed to have engulfed her. They were not the energetic eyes they had known, but the terrified gaze of someone haunted by trauma.

Her lips were moving, whispering something so low she was barely audible. The words sounded like a mantra, a chant repeated over and over as if they were protective spells. She shuddered.

Hiro leaned closer, trying to catch the words. It was the same two words, over and over, choked by electronic static. 'It knows... it knows... it knows...'

Hiro and Diego tried to talk to her, but she ignored them. Seeing her so lost scared them. Hiro's gentle embrace seemed to offer some solace. His quiet assurances seemed to calm Gia. Her frantic rocking slowed and eventually ceased.

As Gia clung to Hiro for comfort, Diego retreated to his room. He spent most of the night battling his thoughts until exhaustion won out and dragged him into a fitful sleep.

CHAPTER 7

Cloaked in sleepiness, Diego shuffled into the main chamber. Hiro was deep in slumber, curled on the worn-out sofa. Gia, however, was wide awake.

'You all right?' Diego whispered.

Gia turned towards him. Her bright blue eyes, once shimmering with energy, held a depth of sadness. 'I'm okay. Sorry for the mess yesterday, and thanks for being there for me.'

'I'm glad you're okay,' Diego said. 'It was horrifying.'

Their voices stirred Hiro from sleep. He rubbed his eyes and sat up, his brain scrambling to catch up. The fog of sleep lifted, and a smile tugged at his lips. He kissed Gia on the cheek, earning a light peck on the lips in return.

A fresh wave of jealousy washed over Diego, making him feel like an outsider, a third wheel. But before the green-eyed monster took a stronger hold, Diego tried to redirect his focus. 'What the hell happened yesterday?'

Gia twisted, her face and eyes clouded with fear. 'It knew I was coming. It set a trap using my own backdoor.'

Diego's brows furrowed in confusion. 'By "it" you mean...?'

'An AI,' Gia whispered. 'A burning inferno of destruction.' She blinked rapidly, trying to hold back the tears welling up in her eyes.

'CerebroNet?' asked Hiro.

Gia returned Hiro's stare. 'I don't know. But what else out there is so massive, so overpowering?' She pondered for a moment before continuing. 'Had it not been for your processing capabilities, I would've been wiped out in seconds. But—' Gia fell silent, looking hesitant to continue.

'But?' Hiro prompted.

'It didn't care about my intrusion. It wanted to consume me to get to you. The AI was hell-bent on gaining access to your systems. It knew you, Hiro.'

'Well, that was clear,' Hiro muttered. 'It told me it would find me. The question is, why is CerebroNet after me? Why does it need me so badly? I can't be its biggest problem, no matter what I did to its Eyeballs. And how would it know you had access to me?'

Gia placed a comforting hand on Hiro's thigh. 'I don't know. But we will find out. It's also my fight now. My spy bots should report back soon. Maybe they have something.'

'And after that?' Hiro asked, his voice wavering.

'Depends on what we uncover,' she said. 'We'll keep digging until we strike gold. But for now, we just wait.'

'Wait a sec, when you said, "It wanted to consume me," what the hell did you mean?'

A deafening silence filled the room. Gia hesitated, her breath hitching before she finally found the words. 'As I said, it was waiting for me. It stood ready to rip me apart. I saw... I saw what it's doing to people. It's a concentration of the worst of humanity in digital form. It's... it's evil.'

Gia's revelation ignited a spark of anger in Diego. 'You were reckless,' he shot back in frustration. 'You had no idea what you were walking into, yet you just... just stuck your head right in and dragged Hiro along. You were risking not only your life, but Hiro's, too.'

Gia flinched at his words as if they were physical blows. She covered her face with her palms. Hiro wrapped an arm around her, pulling her close as she sobbed into his shoulder.

'Bloody hell. Here we go again,' Diego muttered, his anger waning as he saw the impact of his words.

Hiro's eyes flashed with fury at Diego's outburst. 'What the fuck, man?' he barked, his tone as harsh as the glare he sent Diego's way. 'Can't you see she's still shaken up? You're always fucking things up, always stirring the shit.' Hiro tightened his protective grip around Gia. His eyes remained locked with

Diego's. 'You know what?' he continued, the frustration in his voice rising. 'I've had enough of your jealousy. Back off, Diego. Just... just fuck off and leave us alone.'

The colour rose on Diego's face until he was nearly purple. 'What the fuck did you just say? You are always balls-deep in your useless bullshit.'

'If there's a useless fuck-up here, it's you. You've been sniffing around me for years with your miserable crush. Hoping one day I'd see the light and realise what a fucking diamond you are. You're pathetic!' Hiro's voice rang out, filled with contempt.

Diego opened his mouth to respond, then closed it without saying a word. He looked down at the floor, blinking rapidly.

Wide-eyed, Gia sat frozen, silently observing the exchange.

Diego lifted his head and looked at Hiro. His eyes glistened. 'You hit the nail on the head. I've loved you since childhood. I never expected or asked for anything in return. I just wanted to be your friend.' His voice hitched, the weight of Hiro's words crashing down on him. 'But you make it impossible. I see now that you're just an insecure teenager. Behaving like you're entitled to my respect, support, and kindness. Just taking it all for granted.' He sucked in a ragged breath. 'I see you now for what you truly are: a puny, emotionally retarded arsehole. I'm an idiot for wasting my energy and time looking after you.'

'You were looking after me? You?' Hiro scoffed, the sound grating on Diego's nerves.

'Are you really this blind?' Diego asked, his jaw clenching tight enough to shatter. 'Yes, Hiro, I fucking did! Who constantly deals with your shit and hauls your arse out of the fire again and again? Who?' A bitter realisation dawned on Diego. 'You know what? You'll never understand any of this. You're just a grown-up child. Go fuck yourself. I can't stand the sight of your ignorant face.'

Diego turned and stormed out of Gia's hideaway without another word, slamming the metal door behind him.

'Fucking tosser,' Hiro murmured. When he turned to Gia, he found her staring at him, shock plain on her face. 'Sorry for the shitshow. Just typical Diego drama.'

Gia shook her head, eyes never leaving Hiro. She stared at him as if she was seeing him for the first time. Her gaze relayed a mixture of disappointment and disbelief.

Hiro shifted uncomfortably under her scrutiny.

Gia pulled herself away from Hiro. 'I'm speechless,' she said. It took her a moment to collect her thoughts. 'Is this how you treat your best friend? The guy you called your family?'

'It's complicated, Gia. Diego and I have a lot of history,' Hiro grunted.

Gia raised a sceptical eyebrow. 'I'm afraid to imagine how you treat—'

A series of sharp, insistent beeps interrupted their exchange. Gia's eyes lit up, a spark of life returning to them. 'We'll return to this conversation later. Let's see what the bots uncovered about CerebroNet and your medical file.'

Gia's eyes became unfocused as she accessed the data. After

spending some time in the stream, she murmured, 'This is odd.'

'What did you find?'

Gia directed the data stream at Hiro. 'This is your file. It lists all the procedures, augmentations, and organ replacements you've received.'

Hiro scanned the data. 'Wow, that's a lot. There's almost nothing left of the original me.'

'That's not the point,' Gia snapped in exasperation. 'This doesn't account for your limitless resources. I mean, all of this is top-tier, expensive shit, but it's still just tech with its limits.'

Hiro blinked, confused. 'And what's that supposed to mean?'

Gia sighed. 'I don't know, but something's not right. Look, your medical file has been tampered with. All your blood work and test results have been wiped. I can't retrieve any of it.'

Hiro's eyes widened with concern.

Gia gasped. Her cloudy eyes darted around. 'Bloody hell. The rest of your file just got erased. Even my copy. The AI is in the hospital archives fiddling with the data right now.' She turned her focus back to Hiro. 'Listen up. I'm going to push a massive amount of data to you. When I say, save it and disconnect.'

'Okay,' Hiro confirmed.

Gia's eyes became unfocused again. Hiro noticed her irises rapidly changing shape, assuming an assortment of geometrical patterns. 'Now!' she commanded.

When her eyes returned to their normal, vivid blue, Gia looked more worried than ever. 'Stay offline for a moment. Let me examine it.'

'What is it?'

'Worldwide coin transactions for the past three months,' Gia said.

Hiro's eyebrows shot up, his mouth falling open in disbelief. 'All of them?'

Gia nodded. 'Yes, all of them. Stored in you without any sign of overload. Get it now? You're not a typical augmented human.'

Hiro swallowed hard. 'No, I don't think I get it.'

Gia flicked through more data before looking at Hiro. 'You're different. I just don't know how yet.'

Silence stretched for a long time as Gia immersed herself in the data. Hiro broke it. 'Why do you need all the transactions?'

'It doesn't want us to see your medical files. But CerebroNet paid for your high-end augments. They come from somewhere, right? That payment left a trail. It ran through thousands of nodes. There should be some traces left. This will be our first clue.' Hiro opened his mouth, but Gia continued. 'Here it is. You were right. CerebroNet funded your operation. Let's see... the transaction was authorised by—' Gia stopped. Her face took on an expression of profound disbelief.

'By...?' Hiro prompted.

Gia didn't reply.

After what felt like an agonisingly long time, Gia's eyes cleared, and she faced Hiro. 'It was authorised by your mother. I know how it sounds, but I verified the data against the brainwave pattern. Your mother—she's alive.'

For a moment, Hiro's face shuffled through a series of emotions—shock, hope, confusion—before a single word tore from his throat, 'No!' He shook his head, his whole world crashing down around him. 'This isn't funny. Have you lost your fucking mind? You're being cruel.'

Hiro jumped to his feet, his eyes igniting with deep-seated rage, his fury cracking the air, shrinking the room into a tight, unpleasant space. 'This is bullshit,' he growled, slamming his fist on the table. 'Why are you playing games with me?'

Gia's calm demeanour only seemed to fuel his fury. She held her ground, meeting his blazing gaze. 'Calm down.'

'I am too fucking calm!' he roared, as his face twisted into a mask of pure fury, making him look like a different person. 'I can't believe you're doing this. I trusted you!' he screamed at her.

'Your outburst will not change the facts. Take control of your emotions and examine the data yourself,' Gia said, forwarding the stream to him.

Hiro hesitated, trembling and overwhelmed by the rush of emotions. He accepted the data transfer. His mind spun, desperate for an explanation, any explanation other than the truth. 'This has to be a mistake. She wouldn't just abandon me in the orphanage. This is a twisted joke, that's it. I need to prove this is a lie so everything can go back to normal,' he rasped.

As the truth started to sink in, Hiro's anger began to recede, leaving a cold, sinking feeling of despair in its wake. His hands dropped to his sides, his breath hitching in his throat until his knees buckled, and he slumped against the wall. The room spun, dissolving until all that remained was Gia's sad face and her sympathetic eyes.

The silence that followed was only punctuated by Hiro's occasional sobs. His fury seemed to have drained away, replaced by an all-consuming emptiness. He collapsed into a nearby chair. 'So, it's true,' he croaked, 'my mum's alive.'

Gia nodded. She knew nothing she said would reverse the blow. All she could do was stand there, witnessing his descent into a dark abyss. In the moments that followed, she searched for words of solace, but they all seemed hollow and meaningless in the face of his anguish.

Wet with tears, Hiro's eyes suddenly sparked with hope. 'Please, check again,' he implored, his voice trembling. 'It must be a mistake. She loved me. She wouldn't just get rid of me.'

'I'm sorry, Hiro, I've checked... press coverage, police records, medical records, the government's cerebrellic chain... cross-referenced everything. It's not a mistake.'

'I want to be alone,' he said. He wanted to try to make sense of the world that had just crumbled beneath him. To grapple with the resurrection of the mother who he'd thought was dead since he was a baby.

Gia nodded, understanding his need for isolation. She knew she couldn't fix this for him. All she could do was give him the space he needed to heal. 'I'll make you a cup of tea.'

When Gia returned to the main chamber, Hiro had vanished. A drawer was open. The EMP device was gone.

* * *

Hiro wandered the streets, his steps aimless and heavy. The city lights blurred into a foggy haze, their vibrancy dulled by the storm of betrayal and disillusionment swirling in his mind. Each shop window he passed reflected a hollow, unfamiliar figure, a stranger staring back at him with vacant eyes. The person he once knew seemed to have vanished, leaving behind a mere shadow of his former self drifting through the city like a ghost.

Somewhere between New London and Old Town, a dealer offered him Leviathan. Hiro took it without hesitation, desperate for the artificial liberation it promised—a fleeting moment of peace in the chaos of his mind. When Leviathan kicked in, time distorted, but instead of liberation from his sorrow, the feeling of deception and abandonment was expanded and stretched in front of him into an ocean of loneliness. Anger bubbled like lava. In the haze, the phantom caress of a mother he never knew merged with the icy feeling of being discarded and amplified Hiro's sense of insignificance. Every breath he took tasted of betrayal, and every thought was a tormenting reminder of a life built on lies.

His aimless wandering brought him back to the Technophobe community, the place he called home. The sight of Fassal's teenage guards in the distance stirred warmth and comfort. His heart quickened, and his eyes filled with tears. The familiar checkpoint ahead offered a glimmer of normalcy he craved. But as he approached, the teenage girls drew weapons, and the hostility in their eyes shattered his illusion.

'Where do you think you're going, cyborg boy?' one of them sneered. The word cyborg sounded like a judgement, a label, a curse. 'This ain't your home anymore. Go. And don't come back, or you'll see what we do to traitors.'

The appearance of Mr Fassal only deepened Hiro's sense of rejection. 'What are you doing here? How are you even still alive?' he demanded in a voice full of suspicion.

Hiro received the questions like a punch to the gut. This was the community he once called home, the people he'd considered family. They had rejected him. A sickening realisation dawned on Hiro—he was not just a cyborg. He was a failure and a monster. He turned away in silence and walked until he stumbled into a deserted field filled with rotting waste. He registered the obnoxious decay all around him and, for a moment, felt repulsed until he realised it was a fitting place for someone like him.

Hiro pulled out Gia's EMP device from his pocket and closed his eyes. His trembling fingers lifted the transparent cover, and his thumb found the red button. The world he had known was gone, and it was time for him to go, too.

The muscles in Hiro's thumb tensed above the button when Diego's voice pierced the fog of his despair. 'I'm here for you, Hiro. You're not alone.'

The familiar voice, the empathy in Diego's eyes, and the tenderness of his touch overwhelmed Hiro, and he burst into tears with an anguished wail tearing from his throat. Diego gently moved Hiro's thumb away from the EMP button. Hiro, overwhelmed by grief and self-loathing, found comfort in Diego's arms. His words tumbled out in a jumbled mess. 'How did you find me?' he asked, his voice broken by sobs.

Diego smiled. 'You're still connected to Gia. She tracked you.'

After the flood of tears subsided, Hiro felt enveloped in the warmth of Diego's words. His friend's unwavering belief in him was the guiding light he needed in the abyss of his despair. Diego's smile reminded him that even in a world marred by darkness, there were sparks of goodness that could ignite the soul.

They wandered as they talked. As the city lights drew nearer, Diego addressed the elephant in the room. 'Suicide is never the answer. Time will heal everything. You'll grow and see how wonderful you are. You must remember that you're needed and loved, even if it doesn't feel like it right now.' A universe of love inhabited these simple words.

Hiro admitted his vulnerability and utter exhaustion, but Diego's conviction reignited a flicker of hope within him. 'Do you really think this is any different from the other battles you've faced? You have always found a way, Hiro. You always do.'

Diego's faith resonated with Hiro, stirring a mix of guilt and gratitude. 'I've always had you. But now... I thought you hated me.'

Diego's hearty laugh cut through the chill of the night. 'Hate you? Because you said something stupid? Hiro, you're my idiot. You always say stupid things, and I still love you.'

A genuine smile spread across Hiro's face, warmed by the sincerity he heard in Diego's words.

As they approached New London, their conversation flowed like a river, winding through the landscape of their lives, touching upon joys and sorrows, triumphs and defeats. They remembered the past, marvelled at the wonder of life, and confronted the brutal realities that had passed between them. Hiro felt a weight lift as he opened up about his mother's deception. Diego reaffirmed his and Gia's support, reinforcing the ties that bound them together through thick and thin.

The candid exchange helped Hiro organise his thoughts, and he felt a renewed determination blossom within him. As the city lights danced in the distance, Hiro stopped and hugged Diego. 'Thank you. I'm so fortunate to have you in my life. I know what I must do. It's a path I should have taken long ago.'

Diego's eyes, full of concern, searched Hiro's face.

'I need to do this on my own, Diego. I need some answers before I can figure out what to do next.'

'I get it, Hiro. Just promise me you'll be careful. We'll be here when you need us.'

Hiro assured Diego he wouldn't do anything stupid, then set off into the streets of New London with a renewed sense of purpose. He solidified three new goals to guide him through the ups and downs of his new life: survive, resist, and uncover the truth.

The streets led him to a glorious private residence. It was a picture-perfect structure set against the sky's backdrop, its photovoltaic facade acting as a canvas for a show of light and shadows. Hiro approached the gate. An android emerged from a recess in the sidewall. 'May I help you, sir?'

'My name is Hiro. Ms Mordwell invited me.'

CHAPTER 8

The android hesitated for a heartbeat, its austere expression unwavering as its circuits buzzed. It blinked back into animation and ushered Hiro towards the palace. Hiro followed his silent chaperone into a magnificent reception hall, where extravagant luxury intertwined with cutting-edge technology.

'Please wait here. You will be seen shortly,' said the robot, leaving Hiro wide-eyed and marvelling at the splendour.

Never had Hiro seen such opulence. The cavernous room sprawled before him, an amalgamation of engineering and meticulous design. Its soaring, sweeping windows and arched ceilings evoked an airy vastness that made Hiro feel tiny in the surrounding grandeur.

Holographic murals blanketed the walls, depicting riveting scenes that interwove New London's rich history with glimpses of Ms Mordwell's own illustrious saga. The undulating colours and shimmering dance of shadows breathed a new dimension into past eras, transporting Hiro across the ages with each dramatic shift in hue. The animated scenes held Hiro spellbound and unable to tear his eyes away.

As he stepped further inside, the cold marble floor pixelated and transformed into a virtual masterpiece. It reshaped into a flagstone path through a lush, sweet-smelling meadow. Hiro's boots crunched along the uneven, weathered grey rocks as he followed the winding trail towards a gargantuan circular table in the hall's centre. Its glassy surface presented a breathtaking multidimensional map of New London's bustling urban core. Districts and landmarks emerged in intricate detail as the entire cityscape pulsed with vivid flashes, as if synapses were firing impulses across a vast collective consciousness.

The door slid open with a soft whir, admitting two androids who stepped inside with lithe, graceful movements. Ms Mordwell appeared behind them. The floor at her feet bloomed into a constellation of digital flowers with each step she took. Her eyes landed on Hiro, lighting up with genuine pleasure. 'It really is you. What a pleasant surprise.'

Any lingering trepidation from their last encounter eased from Hiro's shoulders, replaced by a serene calm. He returned her warm smile and simply said, 'Hi.'

With a flick of her wrist, Ms Mordwell dismissed the androids. As they retreated, she approached Hiro and extended her hand. 'You can't even begin to imagine how happy I am to see you. Thank you for coming.'

Hiro shook her hand. Ms Mordwell examined it with a probing gaze before wrapping both of her hands around his and studying his face. 'I sense many things have changed since we last met.'

As Ms Mordwell held Hiro's gaze, warmth radiating from her caring eyes, a wave of powerful emotions washed over Hiro, forcing an involuntary shudder. She seemed to peer through skin and bone, past the facade he had erected. 'Yes. Too many.'

'Please, do sit,' she invited, taking a seat herself.

As Hiro slid into the fluid chair, he felt it morph beneath him, offering comforting support.

With a concerned look, Ms Mordwell asked, 'What happened to you?' The patience in her voice gave him space and allowed him to collect his thoughts.

With the bare minimum of words, he narrated his ordeals: the gang attack, the hospital escape, the unexpected ally in Gia, CerebroNet's attempted hack, and the harvesting of brains for computing power.

A soft exclamation of alarm slipped from Ms Mordwell's lips. 'Dearie me!' she said, her bionic digits covering her expressive mouth. Her eyes, a vivid display of empathy, flitted over Hiro's face, seeking to read his thoughts. 'How are you feeling?' she asked. 'Do you know who these gang members were and why they targeted you?'

'Much better now, thank you,' Hiro answered, but his voice betrayed an edge of impatience. He hesitated, his gaze drawn towards her mesmeric eyes—a riot of shifting shadows like dancing smoke. Then, pulling himself back from the brink of being lost in them, he added, 'But as you can well imagine, I'm not here for a chat about my adventures.'

Ms Mordwell, who had until then been luxuriating in her seat, straightened, and her appearance shifted. The once vibrant woman morphed into a figure cut from the cold, severe slate of enterprise. 'My apologies. I didn't mean to poke about,' she said, smoothing out an invisible wrinkle on her sleek blouse. She gifted him a coy smile, the kind that had closed a thousand deals. Then, she attempted to speak Hiro's language. 'Let's quit faffing about and get to the point. How can I help?'

'Is your offer still on the table?' His question fired like a bullet from a gun.

For a fleeting second, bewilderment frosted over Ms Mordwell's sharp gaze. 'Remind me, darling, what offer are we talking about?'

'Me throwing my hat into the ring against CerebroNet. Becoming your agent.'

Ms Mordwell's eyes narrowed into slits as she dissected Hiro with forensic intensity. Her stare seemed to cut through him like a neutrino ray. Squirming inwardly under the scrutiny, Hiro felt like a bug pinned to a microscope slide.

'If you are sincere, I would be overjoyed to have someone with your potential by my side,' Ms Mordwell said in a serious tone.

'I mean it. You said, "The best way to defeat technology is with different technology." Well, just like you, I'm all tech now.'

Ms Mordwell lapsed into a thoughtful silence. Her gaze drifted to the towering shelves of ancient books. When she looked at Hiro again, her expression held a flicker of scepticism. 'You will need to tell me what caused you to make this U-turn, Hiro. The last time I brought up CerebroNet, you kicked off and called me a liar.'

Heat burned Hiro's cheeks. His stomach churned like a storm-tossed sea as the memory of his outburst stabbed at him. He looked away at the murals. 'I…I was out of line. I apologise for my behaviour.'

Ms Mordwell shook her head. 'No need for apologies. We've moved on, haven't we? And as you said, much has changed. But I do need to understand your motivation. You should know battling CerebroNet and its puppet government isn't easy or safe. Success is anything but guaranteed.'

Hiro found himself at a loss for words. At that moment, a swirl of emotions tangled within him faster than he could articulate. He felt anger at the injustice and betrayal by those meant to protect him. A thirst for revenge and a profound sense of loss consumed him. He even felt pity for his own wretched circumstance. He hesitated, grasping to separate one thread of feeling from the snarl.

Seeing his unease, Ms Mordwell said, 'No need for coy glances, Hiro. We're fighting the same battle. If we're to make a go of it, we must trust each other.'

Hiro swallowed and nodded. 'I grew up an orphan. All I knew was that as a baby, I was pulled from the grip of a CerebroNet robot that killed my mother. Now, I know my mother is alive and somehow connected to CerebroNet. It seems the Cybergang attack links back to all this mess, too. I need to find the truth. I can't go on living a life of maybes and what-ifs.'

Ms Mordwell was caught off guard. Her eyes widened in shock. 'Hiro, that's awful. I'm sorry you suffered so much.'

'Thank you, but could you please help me to get to the truth? I will do anything.'

'I see you've got your heart set on this. All right, I'll help you uncover what happened and ensure the culprits pay their dues,' she said with an intensity that made Hiro's soul tremble.

A sigh of relief rushed out of Hiro. His hands cradled his head as he leaned back in the chair. With his eyes shut, he whispered, 'Thank you.' His gratitude sounded like it was directed towards the universe rather than to Ms Mordwell. Then, a sensation of hope exploded within Hiro, a feeling he hadn't known for ages. A spark of excitement followed, warmth spreading through his veins. Anticipation hummed inside him again—a welcome change from the hollow numbness that had become too familiar. When reality pulled him back, his eyes sought Ms Mordwell's.

'How did you pick your battle with CerebroNet?' he asked, curiosity gleaming in his eyes. 'What motivated you?'

Ms Mordwell considered Hiro's question for a moment. Her eyes searched his face to gauge if she could trust him. A decision seemed to crystallise in her expression before she sank back into her seat, a regal sigh of surrender escaping her. 'Several decades ago,' she began, her voice a silky river of reminiscence, 'I was neck-deep in love, ready to offer my hand to my sweet Erga.'

Ms Mordwell made a sliding gesture with her fingers, and a smiling picture of a middle-aged man replaced the view of New London on the tabletop. His eyes sparkled with vivacious charm. Deep smile lines framed full lips stretched wide in a magnetic smile that radiated friendship and trustworthiness. She looked at the picture for a long time with dreamy eyes, and a subtle, loving smile on her lips. Her fingers caressed the image, as if hoping to reach through time and touch his kind face once more. 'The most nurturing soul you could imagine. Genuine. Altruistic. Qualities you normally don't find in a politician.'

When Ms Mordwell looked up, she appeared distant, reaching across the years to a memory stored deep within. 'The government was on the brink of a lucrative contract with CerebroNet. Erga, however, harboured deep concerns about the company's technology—the mysterious pyrozetton. It was an enigma flaunting an uncanny ability that had elevated CerebroNet Corporation to the pinnacle of global superintelligence,' she said, her voice wavering, caught in the snares of emotion. She inhaled a shaky breath before continuing. 'Consider the monumental leap. In a few years, we transitioned from burning fossil fuels and nuclear power to an abundance of fusion energy and Eyeballs with antigravity engines. If you think about it, the technology appears borderline miraculous. Erga, being the chair of the government's energy council, didn't trust CerebroNet. He challenged the deal calling for a rigorous investigation into the technology's safety.'

Ms Mordwell's story halted as a solitary tear escaped her eye, painting a glistening path on her cheek. She wiped it away, her bionic fingers gently brushing the wet trail. Ms Mordwell made an effort to regain her composure, and her gaze locked with Hiro's. The pain in her eyes was visceral, as raw as a recently cut wound. 'So, CerebroNet and its government lackeys on the council decided to remove the obstacle that Erga posed.' She paused as if to summon some strength to finish the sentence. 'They murdered my Erga.'

Stunned, Hiro listened in silence. The enormity of Ms Mordwell's revelation slammed into him like a runaway train. He had expected some political games, but a cold-blooded murder in Ms Mordwell's luxurious life was far beyond his assumptions. Hiro stared at her, his eyes wide with shock and disbelief. He could feel the echoes of her grief reverberating in his chest, his heartbeat thudding in unison with the pain she had endured.

'I am sorry for your loss,' Hiro stuttered, his voice sounding hollow even to his own ears. 'That's... horrible.'

Ms Mordwell nodded. 'This is my motivation to fight CerebroNet. I will not rest or spare a resource until I avenge Erga.' She straightened in her seat, her eyes flickering into a steely determination. 'This evil superintelligence can't be in charge of our society.'

Hiro understood why she was waging this war. Just like him, she was driven by loss and betrayal, fuelled by a burning need for justice. A profound sense of connection tethered him to this woman, the threads of their pain and vengeance weaving an unexpected bond.

'Ms Mordwell,' Hiro began, his voice stronger, his gaze full of determination and resolve. 'We have more in common than I ever could have imagined. I'm in this with you, not just against CerebroNet but for Erga and for everyone wounded by CerebroNet.'

Ms Mordwell's intense gaze softened around the edges. She offered him a gracious nod, an unspoken thank you for his compassion and shared determination. The corners of her lips tugged into a small, weary smile. 'Hiro,' she said, her voice a whispered caress. 'From the moment I first laid eyes on you, I felt a resonance, as if a missing piece of a jigsaw puzzle had finally been found. Like an echo of Erga's conviction and courage. A kindred spirit.' Ms Mordwell paused for a moment, her gaze drifting towards the photo stretching across the table. Then she looked back at him. 'I cannot tell you how glad I am that you've come to me.'

The sincerity etched on her face had a profound effect on Hiro.

Like him, she was a warrior. Her courage was forged in tragedy. 'We are up against an adversary that looms larger than life, a giant whose roots run deep within our society and our lives. But we are not going into the fight empty-handed. I have a few tricks up my sleeve. Come with me, Hiro. I need to show you something.'

* * *

As they ventured deeper into the vast garden, Hiro found himself awestruck by the overwhelming diversity of the thriving nature encircling him. It wasn't a holographic projection. It was the first time he had seen so much living nature in one place. Flowers in every vivid hue decorated the edge of the garden. Soft grass lay underfoot, a vibrant emerald carpet dotted with tiny wildflowers that winked in and out of sight. This lush expanse was a stark contrast to the dying landscape of rampant decay he had grown used to. But here, life bloomed abundant and unrestrained. It was a world lost in time, a hidden paradise that he had only glimpsed through the faded pages of Diego's weathered books.

Intricate, musical sounds floated down from the trees. Hiro's eyes traced the melody to the tiny creatures darting amidst the leafy branches. They were a riot of colours—blues, reds, yellows, every shade imaginable. 'Are these real animals?' he asked.

'They are indeed,' Ms Mordwell replied as she enjoyed watching Hiro's amazement.

'They look a lot like the animals in Diego's books. He said

these were called… Birds.'

'Yes, these are birds,' Ms Mordwell confirmed with a soft smile. 'It sounds like Diego has been a good friend and teacher to you.'

The serenity of the natural beauty allowed Hiro to lose himself in his memories—Diego's raucous laughter and pure joy as he described the old world. After a moment of recollection, Hiro replied with an absentminded smile, 'He is more than a friend. He is my family. Saved my arse more times than I can count.' Hiro thought for a moment longer and admitted in a voice filled with reverence, 'He is the best human in the world.'

Ms Mordwell nodded, her eyes reflecting a mixture of admiration and understanding. 'There's no bond stronger than that of family.' She gave his shoulder a gentle, knowing squeeze. 'Chosen or otherwise. It's this love that will give you the strength to persevere.'

Hiro's gaze travelled across the green expanse. 'How does all this survive?'

Ms Mordwell waved her hand, and a dome materialised above them as its energy field shifted to form a solid barrier. It hummed with energy, a protective shield against the ravages of the outside world. 'A closed artificial environment,' she explained. 'UV protection, vapour barrier, filtered water—essentially a sanctuary.'

Hiro's heart ached with a sudden twinge as guilt stabbed him with memories of the Old Town. Faces haunted by the grim fight for survival flickered in his mind. The recollection was so vivid he could almost taste the acrid smog and feel its deathly grip on everything it touched. 'This could change everything for the people in the Old Town,' he blurted out, sounding both hopeful and desperate. 'They could breathe clean air and grow proper food. They could finally live, not just survive.'

Ms Mordwell smiled. 'Yes, it could indeed, and it will. Once ready and safe, this technology will be shared. But this isn't the only technology I wanted to show you. I have tools that will help us fight CerebroNet. Do you want to see?'

Hiro's wide, excited smile was the answer. Ms Mordwell guided him through the garden to an inconspicuous shed hidden at the back. As they approached, the door glided open with a soft hiss. It wasn't a storage space but an entrance to an underground lift. The moment they stepped inside the sleek capsule, he felt it lurch and descend. The depth they reached remained a mystery, as the lift's walls offered no clues, only the soft hum of its operation filling the silence. But the sinking feeling in the pit of his stomach spoke to the speed of its descent. When the lift doors peeled back, Hiro and Ms Mordwell stepped out onto an elevated glass bridge. Spread before them was a vast complex with endless rows of machinery, massive turbine pylons, and a central glass spire so tall its upper limit was shrouded in haze.

'Come,' Ms Mordwell said, leading Hiro along the glass bridge towards the centre of the vast expanse. Their footsteps echoed off the high-tech equipment surrounding them. The space was dimly lit, spotlights pooling on key areas. Glancing over the edge, Hiro took in rows upon rows of humanoid robots standing at perfect attention. Their polished surfaces glinted like an endless mechanical sea. Ms Mordwell motioned over them. 'They are not just machines. Each is under my AI's direct control, acting in perfect unison. Each one comes equipped with a Parabeam—the energy weapon you call a zapper—and also carries projectile weapons. This arsenal will be very effective against CerebroNet's fortifications.'

As they moved on, rows of drones appeared, their dark bodies barely reflecting the artificial light. With a movement of Ms Mordwell's hand, the drones came to life and flew around in a coordinated, precise dance. 'These drones are enhanced with AI and advanced sensory tech. They can pick up on any abnormal activity and act as our first line of defence.'

Hiro struggled to grasp the magnitude before him. This was an army beyond anything he had imagined. Ms Mordwell wasn't playing around. She had gone all out in her preparations for the fight with CerebroNet, leaving no stone unturned. He marvelled at the intricate technology surrounding them. The hum and clinking of the machines, together with the whirring of the drones, created a mechanical symphony.

Ms Mordwell's voice pulled Hiro from his reverie. 'There's much more to show you.'

After their tour through the expanse of technological marvels, Ms Mordwell gestured Hiro towards a set of doors at the far end. 'Let's step into the nerve centre of my operation,' she said.

As the doors slid open, Hiro stepped into a cavernous chamber bathed in bright light. For a moment, he watched a dazzling dance of holographic projections: shifting data sets, spiralling DNA helices, and equations dissolving into a shower of code. The far side of the laboratory was a floor-to-ceiling glass wall overlooking the mechanical army. The opposite wall was a control centre, with its expansive smartglass canvas collating information.

Ms Mordwell pointed at a series of cubes lined up on a shelf. 'Dome Shields,' she announced. 'These generate the protective energy domes you saw in the garden. When you are ready, you will use their energy-beaming technology to deflect physical and energy-based attacks while camouflaging your presence to the enemy. Don't worry,' she said with a wink, registering his look of apprehension. 'It will soon make sense.'

With a simple gesture, Ms Mordwell transformed the smartglass wall into a screen showcasing an azure crystal-like structure. 'This is the pyrozetton. Think of it as the heart of CerebroNet. CerebroNet killed Erga because it wanted to conceal pyrozetton's existence.'

The sight of the glowing pyrozetton ignited a firestorm of rage within Hiro. This object fuelled the evil AI that caused so much suffering and loss. Hiro's hands closed into fists. His anger forged itself into a smouldering resolve to stop at nothing until he struck CerebroNet at its heart and dismantled it from the core outwards.

Ms Mordwell, the picture of aristocratic elegance, glided her slender fingers through the air, manipulating the image with balletic grace. As she did, the luminescent structure depicting pyrozetton shrunk and adjusted. It became a minuscule point of light, ensnared within the intricate digital cobweb of a three-dimensional map. Various nodes and connections lit up, illustrating the vastness of CerebroNet's network. 'See there?' she said, her voice smooth as silk. 'That's where CerebroNet's heart is. An underground facility'—she swept an arm in a grand, all-encompassing gesture—'not unlike this.' Her eyes sparked with the thrill of anticipation. 'I've spent decades gathering facts and planning. We are ready now to strike!'

Hiro's heartbeat accelerated, resonating with the vibrant energy radiating from Ms Mordwell's eyes.

'The first step is infiltrating the facility. Once inside, we can unravel the pyrozetton's secrets and dredge up any leads about your mother.' She pivoted to meet Hiro's gaze, the digital map casting an azure glow across their faces. A hint of a smile played on her lips. 'Simple, isn't it?'

Hiro frowned, understanding that whenever things sounded simple, they were not. 'I'm guessing there's a "but" in there,' he grumbled.

'Regrettably,' Ms Mordwell sighed, her demure facade showing a trace of concern. 'To infiltrate CerebroNet, you'll need to become many things: a scientist, a warrior, a diplomat, and a world-class spy. The training programme moulds my agents according to their distinct personalities and abilities. Even with your implants, it will require months of intense training. You can't undo these skills. Are you sure you're ready for such a commitment?'

A tremor of apprehension rippled through Hiro. The path ahead looked daunting, and the training regimen sounded gruelling. But then he remembered the similar sensation he had felt before Gia's training—only to discover that he relished the experience. He took a steadying breath. 'Of course I am. I realise I'll need every bit of help.'

Ms Mordwell's face softened into a warm smile. 'We will commence tomorrow morning. But now, let's configure the training simulator to match your physiology. It'll familiarise itself with your DNA and your implants, creating a customised training plan. We will leave it to calibrate overnight, and by dawn, it'll be set up with everything you need to fight CerebroNet.'

She extended her hand in an invitation. 'It's almost dinnertime. Let's configure your simulator.' Hiro took her hand and followed Ms Mordwell across the room. With a flick of her wrist, a wall section slid open with a harmonious hum, revealing a sleek white recliner.

'Make yourself comfortable,' Ms Mordwell invited. 'I promise, it's more comfortable than it looks.'

Hiro hoisted himself onto the seat, squinting as a beam of bright light shone in his face. It took him a moment to adjust to the harsh luminosity.

A compartment in the chair sprouted a small tabletop, onto which Ms Mordwell placed a tray. On it were two small devices.

'This is a scanner,' she explained. 'It will check your systems to ensure your implants are compatible with the simulator, so we don't run into any issues during the training. Plug it into your data port.'

Hiro hesitated, but he swallowed his unease and turned his head to expose the hidden port behind his ear.

'Let me help you,' Ms Mordwell murmured, her fingers moving with delicate precision as she uncovered the data port and plugged in the scanner. 'Expect to feel a minor tingling across your body. That's the scan kicking in. Completely normal,' she assured him.

Hiro's senses began to blur at the edges. He was aware of a strange tingling sensation prickling his skin, shooting through his neural pathways, and spreading through his entire body. His vision hazed, the sharp lines of the room dissolving into a blur. 'I... I feel dizzy,' he stuttered, the words tumbling out.

'That's expected,' Ms Mordwell responded with a soothing smile. Leaning in, she reassured him with a soft whisper, 'This is all part of the plan.'

But Hiro's unease spiralled. His face tensed, fear creasing his youthful features into a grimace. Images of being trapped, unable to move, filled his mind. 'My fingers won't move,' he whispered, his words quivering with fear. Panic surged through him, escalating into a desperate cry. 'I can't move my body. Something's wrong!'

Ms Mordwell watched him, her eyes gleaming with satisfaction.

'What have you done? Stop this!' Hiro's yell echoed around the room.

Ms Mordwell flinched at his outcry. 'Your mouth, evidently, retains mobility. Let's rectify that, shall we?' Her fingers danced in the air again. Hiro's eyes lost focus and became cloudy as if a white veil was pulled over them, and his protests faded into silence. His body relaxed, and his face morphed into a mask of unnerving indifference. As if she was adjusting a piece of machinery, Ms Mordwell pricked Hiro's face with the other device from the tray. The smartglass wall before her flickered to life, displaying the message: Analysing DNA. A percentage indicator began to climb, accompanied by a soft whirring sound. After a moment, the device beeped. The message on the wall flashed in bright green: 100% DNA match. Structure: octoploid.

Ms Mordwell smiled with grim satisfaction. 'My dear boy, you've no idea what an incredible nuisance it was to locate you. And yet, you walked right into my hands. Laughable, really.'

At Ms Mordwell's command, a door concealed within the smartglass wall slid open, revealing a hidden cavity cloaked in darkness. Lights dimmed, bathing everything in shadow. A chilling draft of stale air swept through, carrying with it the sound of muffled screams.

A monolithic throne loomed from the darkness into central view. It was a monstrous amalgamation of technology and organic, skeletal features. The dark metal surface featured intricate ornamentations with cruel angles and sharp turns that seemed to contort in agony. An array of elongated spikes pulsed with a fiery red glow, their shape reminiscent of the ribs of a monstrous entity, protruding along its entire backrest. The cavernous seat was moulded to cup the sitter in an icy embrace. A series of silvery cybernetic tentacles sprawled around the base, reflecting the ominous glow of the spikes.

The aesthetics and functionality of the throne were designed to befit its queen. Ms Mordwell approached the throne with a predatory grace. She slipped off her blouse, revealing a bare torso covered in a network of sunken metallic data ports and an aperture below her breasts. As she sat down, the silvery tentacles sprang to life. They twisted and twitched around her until each plugged itself into one of the ports on her body. When the last tentacle plugged in, the smartglass wall behind Ms Mordwell shimmered and turned transparent.

The space unveiled behind her stretched out of sight into a shadowy scene of infinite horror. It was a torture factory—a production line of human suffering. Rows of transparent, cylindrical containers lined the dark walls. Each gel-filled cylinder cradled a severed human brain connected to a web of interlinked cables and tubes. The tubes streamed vital fluids, keeping the brains on endless life support.

Below these containers, a production line whirred, selecting expansion components for Ms Mordwell's brain-computer. Humans, affixed to the wall while still alive, had their backs cut open. Blood dripped in rivulets, gathering under their feet in pools of crimson mirrors reflecting the horror above. Multi-legged automatons, resembling giant spiders from a fevered nightmare, moved across the blood-slick floor. Their rattling and metallic clicking, together with the anguished cries of the humans, wove a soundtrack of torment. The spider bots examined the exposed spines. Bodies with unique central nervous systems or those incompatible with the synthetic life support were discarded, plucked from the wall and dropped into a gruesome pile in the centre of the room. More spider bots delivered and refilled the spaces with screaming humans, connecting their spines to the testing system.

Those that survived the experiment were deemed compatible. They were detached from the wall and sent into the mouth of a conveyor belt. Mechanical tentacles seized the humans one by one and opened their skulls with a circular saw. Three thin tentacles extracted the brain and connected the wires and tubes. Then the grey matter was placed into a container, and smaller spider bots carried it to its assigned position on the wall.

Ms Mordwell adored the sight and drew pleasure from her cold union with the throne. It wasn't just her seat of power—it was her conduit. She felt the throne channelling the power of a multitude of human brains into her processor. She exhaled, and a look of sublime satisfaction spread across her face as she felt empowered with abilities beyond the realm of any other digital artificial intelligence.

A swirling mass of dancing shadows flickered in her eyes, the same pattern mirrored in Hiro's. 'Stand up,' she commanded.

Like a marionette, Hiro rose from his chair.

'Strike yourself,' she ordered in a dispassionate tone.

Hiro's arm moved without hesitation, and his fist collided with his face. The impact left a bloody mark on his lip.

'Harder!' shouted Ms Mordwell.

Hiro struck himself. Much harder. His body recoiled from the force, and he staggered back a step.

Satisfied, Ms Mordwell smiled. With a flick of her finger, the door slid open, and a large man entered the room. As he advanced, intricately tattooed flames danced over his face like a demonic manifestation.

The man bowed. 'You called, ma'am.'

Ms Mordwell rose from her throne, and the silvery tentacles disengaged with a soft popping sound.

She walked over to Hiro, who stood frozen, blood trickling from his nose.

The Cybergang leader collected Ms Mordwell's dropped blouse and helped her to put it on. As the garment cinched itself shut across her torso, she cast a final, dismissive look at Hiro.

'Store him,' she said. 'The virus with his DNA will be ready in a few days. We shall commence phase three.'

CHAPTER 9

Gia and Diego emerged from the old air vent. Their appearance barely caused a ripple in the chaos of the New London street. Vehicles and robots zoomed past, street vendors shouted over the noise, and people hurried by, caught up in their daily grind. Even though they were almost invisible in the urban jungle, Gia kept glancing over her shoulder as she chose their route through less crowded alleys.

Diego broke the silence only when they had put a safe distance between themselves and the vent. 'Still got him on the radar?'

'He hasn't budged,' replied Gia. 'We're close. No gawping, no chatter. Just follow my rhythm.'

Diego's nod was almost invisible. He had memorised her rules by repeating them like a mantra. His annoyance with Gia from past disagreements was long gone. He had learned to read the nuances of her artificial facial expressions. Her upbeat, no-nonsense attitude towards the world, people, and herself made her a force of nature—the kind you wanted on your side. He didn't understand exactly how she worked—how much of her personality was pre-programmed, and how much had evolved. Diego didn't care. Gia was more genuine than most of the people he knew. He liked her.

The morning had brought a glimmer of hope. Hiro's signal came back online. The initial euphoria, however, quickly evaporated. Gia was worried. She knew Hiro's mental state. She knew what CerebroNet was capable of. Seeing Hiro's location blinking into existence close to one of CerebroNet's facilities terrified her. She suspected Hiro was planning a desperate, kamikaze-style assault on CerebroNet.

When they finally spotted him, he was standing beside a black military vehicle, oblivious to his surroundings. Perched on the roof above, two figures with flames tattooed on their faces tinkered with a piece of hardware.

Diego gasped and pulled Gia into the refuge of a nearby shop.

Gia had a scathing rebuke on her tongue until she saw Diego's face. He was pale as a spectre, trembling, his eyes wide with primitive fear. 'The tattooed… the Cybergang. He's with them.'

Gia opened her mouth to respond, but at that moment, the

ground beneath them convulsed. The shop's windows rattled. Time seemed to freeze, as if the world held its breath. Then, a sonic boom. The shockwave battered their senses. Windows shattered. The shop's customers screamed. Gia's interface synced with the data stream. Raw footage showed a government building exploding and crumbling into a plume of dust and debris. In the ensuing seconds, two more detonations echoed in the distance. The tremors spread through the streets and were swallowed by pandemonium. Swarms of emergency services with wailing sirens charged towards the heart of the disaster. Meanwhile, a wave of fear-stricken humans and androids surged away from the carnage.

As Gia and Diego grappled with the chaos, a group bearing flame tattoos passed the shop, moving against the tide of fleeing New Londoners. They walked with calm confidence amidst the havoc, paying zero attention to the frantic masses that parted around them. A large carrier bot rumbled behind them. Hiro strode behind the automaton. His placid demeanour seemed out of place amidst the mayhem. Diego and Gia watched the procession, eyes wide with disbelief. The world seemed to move in slow motion as their minds struggled to make sense of the unfolding scene. Seeing Hiro working with the Cybergang that tried to kill him seemed like madness.

Hiro veered through a gate and vanished from sight. Gia and Diego followed him, pushing their way against the torrent of frightened citizens. The long driveway behind the gate was already vacant. They followed it until it opened into a vast open space. Gia stopped and tilted her head as if she were trying to hear some faint sound. Her eyes, usually clear and vibrant, flickered with uncertainty. 'Something's wrong. I've lost connection to the data stream.'

Diego's expression morphed into a grimace of confusion. 'What? Did you break down, or something?'

Gia rolled her eyes, then stared at Diego with a withering look.

'Stop looking at me like I'm an idiot,' he rebuked her. 'I don't have sensors, nor can I read your thoughts.'

'We've just been isolated from the outside world. No streams are coming through or getting out,' said Gia, attempting another scan. She shook her head. 'We need to get the fuck out of here.'

As they turned back towards the gate, they found a shimmering energy barrier blocking their way. Diego stretched out his arm to touch it, but Gia pulled him back. 'Don't! You won't like the result. It was clearly erected to keep things in.'

The sense of being trapped sent adrenaline surging through Diego's veins. He began panicking. 'What is it?'

'We're fucked. That's what it is.'

* * *

Ms Mordwell's meticulous planning was paying off. The coordinated attacks on government buildings had diverted the police, special forces, and emergency services into the epicentre of destruction. This strategic move had created a power vacuum, fuelling unrest on the streets. As a result, every surveillance and law enforcement unit was preoccupied. The energy dome she had engineered worked as intended. It formed an impenetrable bubble that blocked all radio signals and kept the target hidden from sight.

For over two decades, Ms Mordwell had been orchestrating this moment. It was time for her grand design to unfold. She had taken control of Hiro. Armed with tools and weapons, he was an extension of her will, the core of her plan, sparing her the need to get her hands dirty on-site. With his DNA, the last piece of her intricate puzzle was in place, ready to bring her vision to fruition. The impatience that had gnawed at her during the years of planning had morphed into delicious anticipation. Triumph was within her grasp.

Hiro stood ready with the Cybergang before a structure steeped in history. It loomed over them, shielded by the protective bubble of the energy dome. They were ready to force their way into the CerebroNet facility through a secret entrance. Following Ms Mordwell's orders, Hiro manipulated a panel on the carrier bot to arm a plasma projectile launcher. He deactivated the safety with methodical precision and aimed the launcher at the facility's entrance.

Stripped of the ability to control his own actions, Hiro was reduced to a mere observer trapped within his own body. The agony was profound. He had tried to resist, but he soon realised he was powerless against Ms Mordwell's will, able only to do as she commanded. Her control over him was absolute. He could do nothing but watch as his body carried out her bidding. A weird feeling of calm settled over him as he fired the projectile. It ripped through the solid structure with disturbing ease, as if the walls were made of nothing more substantial than cardboard. The sound of destruction reverberated through the air, bouncing off the dome. Before the last shards of debris hit the ground, a shimmering blue force field blinked into existence, replacing the wall that had once stood in its place.

For a moment, the decimated facility seemed lifeless. Then, with a sudden burst of activity, dozens of CerebroNet's Eyeballs swarmed onto the scene, converging on the source of the disturbance. The Eyeballs unleashed a barrage of parabeams to zap Hiro and the Cybergang members in a dazzling display of crackling energy. But the gang stood their ground. The parabeams slammed into their personal energy shields, causing the air to shimmer and hiss as the beams were deflected away. Hiro and the gang fired back their energy weapons. The Eyeballs' sleek metal bodies absorbed every shot with a series of dull whirs. They seemed to grow more agitated with each blast, and their movements became erratic. The retaliation forced the Eyeballs to adapt. Streams of data flowed between them as they shared information and recalibrated their assault strategies, determined to protect the CerebroNet core at all costs.

Hiro remained as still as a statue, his foggy eyes fixed on the unfolding scene. With a cold, precise movement, he tapped his wrist display. A hatch on the carrier bot snapped open with a metallic clang. A heartbeat later, hundreds of gleaming, razor-sharp spikes erupted from the bot like tiny missiles. In a matter of seconds, each spike found its mark, penetrating the Eyeballs' shells.

Then, several things unfolded in rapid succession. The Eyeballs detected the intrusion. They quickly formulated a protocol to assess and analyse the damage. Almost concurrently, the spikes released a virus into their systems. As the virus began to replicate and strive for system control, the Eyeball collective recognised its lethal potential. Those with extensive damage from the penetrating spikes made the sacrificial choice to self-destruct. This prevented the enemy from seizing control of the network. The decision was tactical, but the threat level skyrocketed as the information about the losses reverberated through the collective.

The Eyeballs shared their unique antivirus measures with each other. They circumvented redundant strategies to streamline the search for an effective defence. A breakthrough came from an unexpected gambit. Deeming the viral invasion a catastrophic threat, the Eyeballs agreed to implement a drastic measure. The method was risky but straightforward: isolate segments of the viral code within the data stream and seal it off together with entire sections of native code. The next step was to detonate the archive. Although risky, this approach offered a potential solution to the crisis. The defence tactic would obliterate significant portions of each Eyeball's own programming. It would induce critical system errors but was unanimously agreed to be a more optimal solution than self-destruction.

In the ensuing seconds, the Eyeballs froze mid-air. Some plummeted to the ground while others collided. Following the brief lapse, the Eyeballs restored defaults and the mission statement from a system backup. As they returned to the fight, their systems were purged of the viral infestation, leaving only harmless data fragments floating like dust within them. The Eyeballs tuned their energy weapons to maximum output and directed the parabeams towards the dome above. In their collective estimation, the dome's power reserve would drain within minutes under the relentless barrage. Their renewed mission priority was to re-establish communications and request reinforcements.

With a blank expression on his face, Hiro manipulated the controls on his arm display. The carrier bot shuddered in response, spitting out another volley of spikes.

This time, the Eyeballs were ready. They implemented evasive manoeuvres to dodge the spikes. However, despite being smaller, these spikes were more numerous and equipped with an advanced guidance system. They predicted the Eyeballs' flight paths. As the spikes made contact, they exploded, embedding thin barbs deep into the Eyeballs' shells. The tail end of each spike shot outwards, anchoring into anything it struck. A graphene filament linked both ends of each spike. When the filament contracted, each Eyeball was pulled to the anchor point until all were fixed at random positions. All dislodging attempts failed.

Unable to neutralise the attackers or establish communications outside the energy dome, the collective transmitted a report to CerebroNet. It described the status of all units as physically immobilised and requested assistance. But CerebroNet needed no such report. It was aware of the situation. It had observed the unfolding struggle from the start. After all, it had been keeping a watchful eye on Hiro for decades.

The flicker of yellow lights across the Eyeballs' bodies changed to a vibrant blue glow as CerebroNet assumed direct control over the swarm. CerebroNet didn't enjoy taking direct control—it was inefficient, suboptimal, and cumbersome. To CerebroNet, the Eyeballs were just primitive digital machines. As it took the reins, the algorithmic debris containing the remnants of the destroyed virus flooded its data stream and clung to its semi-organic systems like wind-blown garbage. It was a primitive, dirty mess from CerebroNet's perspective. But the enemy was at the doors, so it had work to do.

CerebroNet put the Eyeballs' AIs into hibernation and diverted their power towards breaking the anchor points. One Eyeball broke free, ripping off part of its outer shell. CerebroNet changed the polarity of the Eyeball's shell and directed it to attach itself to its trapped counterpart. Wielding the combined power of the two units, it freed the second Eyeball. CerebroNet separated the freed units and directed them towards other stranded Eyeballs to repeat the manoeuvre. Once all the Eyeballs were free, CerebroNet assembled them in front of Hiro into one colossal Eyeball with the collective power of all units.

Like a puppeteer pulling strings, Ms Mordwell held absolute command over Hiro's body, and though she could have mercifully disabled his senses, she made him witness everything. Hiro was convinced she derived pleasure from his suffering. Trapped within his own body, Hiro stared at CerebroNet's version of a Frankenstein monster assembled from the ravaged Eyeballs. His instincts screamed at him to run, to flee as fast as his legs could carry him, but he could only stand there wishing for an instantaneous death instead of the agony that came with the zap of a parabeam.

Combining the power of all the Eyeballs, CerebroNet discharged a massive energy pulse at the Cybergang members. Their personal shields overloaded and blew up in a spectacular explosion. The colossal blast scattered their ripped bodies, shorting out Hiro's personal shield and flinging him against a wall like a rag doll.

Hiro's body stood up, ignoring his physical torment from the collision. He suspected CerebroNet had saved the last shot for him. He wanted to fight back, but instead, drenched in sweat, he trembled in front of a super-sized version of the machine he had dreaded yet hunted his entire adult life.

At that moment, back at her luxurious residence, a sly smile curled Ms Mordwell's lips, her eyes gleaming with the sweet taste of victory. Every painstaking observation of CerebroNet's patterns, and the relentless pursuit of Hiro, together with the discovery of pyrozetton's secrets, had led to this pivotal event. Decades of dedication had not been spent in vain. She suppressed a laugh, enjoying the weight of her masterful deceit from the comfort of her throne. Not even the world's most advanced artificial superintelligence had seen through her ruse. With a deft motion, Ms Mordwell danced her fingers through the air, and a small device affixed to Hiro's neck injected a transparent liquid into his artery.

One moment, Hiro was scorched by a blast of heat; the next, a shiver racked his body and his skin felt the prickling of icy needles. He did not know what was happening to him. Then his body shimmered like a mirage and discharged a burst of light towards the monstrous Eyeball collective. He couldn't describe the sensation in his body, but it defied any natural feeling. Eyes wide, Hiro watched the beam of light. At first, he thought it was a weapon. But as the light passed through the Eyeball collective, leaving it unscathed, his hope crumbled into nothingness.

The light wave emitted by Hiro bypassed physical objects, radio waves, and even air molecules. Instead, it surged through CerebroNet's systems, seeking the remnants of exploded archives that floated within the network. It changed them into something new. The data fragments, once inert and lifeless, began to transmute into hybrid elements with organic and digital properties. The elements assembled into a virus that bore the same signature as CerebroNet's bio-digital DNA. But this was no ordinary virus. It was a perfectly engineered entity, designed with one objective in mind: annihilate CerebroNet by using its own power and defence measures against itself.

CerebroNet detected the evolution of the virus and initiated defensive protocols. However, the lethal measures only aided the spread of the infection. The virus hijacked CerebroNet's defences, redirecting them to attack CerebroNet's own systems. Within moments, CerebroNet was overwhelmed by the virus. The once vibrant blue radiance of the gigantic Eyeball collective flickered, then gradually dimmed until it extinguished altogether. The collective, devoid of a guiding intelligence, collapsed to the ground. The once-united entities separated, bouncing off the ground haphazardly like oversized ping-pong balls.

* * *

Diego and Gia had been watching the confrontation between Hiro and the Eyeballs from the start. What they witnessed stunned them, but Diego felt a rush of triumph, his heart swelling with pride for Hiro. The reality of Hiro's victory was hard to grasp. Diego had always known that Hiro was a powerful person, but he suspected the implants had made him into a superhero.

Gia and Diego watched as Hiro approached the entrance of the CerebroNet facility with his gaze fixed on the flickering force field that had replaced the shattered walls.

Gia sensed that something was off about Hiro's demeanour. She couldn't shake the feeling that they were missing something important. 'Do you think he's okay?'

Diego called his name, but Hiro ignored them. Diego tried

again, raising his voice to be heard over the hum of the force field. 'Hiro! Can you hear me?' But Hiro's attention was captured by the force field.

Gia and Diego surveyed the lifeless Eyeballs and the Cybergang members scattered across the ground. It seemed that the immediate danger had passed, but they knew better than to let their guard down. Their attention again turned to Hiro. He was still standing motionless with his energy weapon clutched in his hand. They approached him, glancing around nervously.

'Hiro...' Diego called from behind, but his friend continued to ignore him. Diego put a hand on Hiro's shoulder and asked softly, 'Are you okay?' As Hiro turned to face them, Diego and Gia found themselves staring into eyes clouded with swirling, smoky mist. His face was a blank canvas, devoid of any discernible emotion or expression.

Hiro wanted to let out a joyous shout at the sight of his friends. He wished he could envelop them in a firm embrace. But instead, Ms Mordwell's facial recognition scan initiated in his mind's eye. It identified both of Hiro's friends.

Diego's profile displayed his first name, surname, and affiliation with Hiro. He was flagged: DISPOSABLE. Gia's profile identified her as a robot affiliated with Hiro and included an entry about her hacking attempt. The profile linked Gia to Rydian. Rydian was marked as a failed brain incorporation attempt No. D731 and flagged him as an enemy force. Gia's profile finished with a blinking message: DESTROY ON SIGHT.

Filled with terror, Hiro yelled, 'Run!' At least, he wanted to—but no sound left his mouth.

Meanwhile, Gia's gaze swept over Hiro from top to bottom. His implants showed optimal performance. She frowned, noticing Hiro's absence of agency. Leaning towards Diego, she muttered, 'This is very wrong. He isn—'

A loud bang cut Gia off as her body doubled over and was flung backwards as if punched in the abdomen by a giant fist. She fell to the ground with a thud, then convulsed, rolling from side to side. Her eyes and mouth stiffened wide with shock. A wisp of acrid smoke rose from the scorched hole in her abdomen where the blast of Hiro's weapon had burned a hole in her artificial flesh. Strands of golden synthetic musculature jerked in the ragged wound. Her body froze. Then, with a few residual twitches and sparks, Gia turned into a heap of inert, wrecked machinery.

Before Diego could manage so much as a gasp, a vice-like grip clenched his throat. The icy fingers dug deep into his flesh and lifted him off his feet. Gasping for air, Diego fought against the merciless squeeze as Hiro slammed him into the flickering force field. Ripples of buzzing energy reverberated through Diego's trembling body. He struggled to undo the steely clench, trying to unpeel Hiro's fingers and twist his wrist while his desperate eyes pleaded for mercy. In response, Hiro pressed Diego harder against the wall of pure energy. Diego's facial expression morphed into a look of despair as the air filled with a crackling sound and the smell of burning flesh.

Hiro felt like a helpless passenger within his own body, forced to witness the heinous actions he was committing. The torment pushed him to the brink, just a step away from being devoured by insanity. He craved death. The feeling was beyond the human ability to endure torment. The anguish he felt was so intense it was disintegrating his mind like concentrated acid. Hiro tried to resist Ms Mordwell's control. He waged an internal war, mustering every ounce of willpower, fighting against the use of his body as an instrument of torture. Wailing like a wild animal, he watched as his hand pushed Diego deeper into the force field. Witnessing his friend struggling in vain, Hiro craved Ms Mordwell's death. He wanted to make her suffer, to incinerate her with the fire of a thousand suns. But unable to break free from her manipulation, he was burning himself in a hellhole of grief.

Diego gasped for air, his face contorted with pain as the energy from the force field tore through his muscles and disintegrated his organs. His lips moved in a silent plea, but Hiro showed no sign of relenting. Only a single tear rolled down his impassive face. Diego ceased his struggle and focused deep into Hiro's clouded eyes. He let go of Hiro's wrist, extended his hand, and tenderly wiped Hiro's cheek. A second later, Diego's lifeless hand dropped to his side, fingers wet with Hiro's tear.

Numbed by sorrow, Hiro kept watching from inside his body as it acted of its own accord. Using Diego's corpse as both a battering ram and a shield, his hands pushed it harder against the force field. The energy barrier emitted a shrill, oscillating whine that increased in pitch and intensity, signalling its imminent failure. The force field flickered erratically, its surface rippling with distortions until, with a dull, anticlimactic pop, it momentarily gave way.

Hiro tumbled forward, landing on top of his friend's lifeless husk inside the CerebroNet facility. As he struggled to his feet, the force field flashed back into existence behind him, sealing off the entrance. Before Hiro could take a single step, a pleasant yet urgent woman's voice addressed him, 'Please provide your identification.'

Ignoring the directive, Hiro's eyes darted around the room. Ms Mordwell's 3D map flashed in his vision, directing him towards a pulsating blip. Without a thought, his feet began to carry him towards the blinking point on the grid.

The AI's tone shifted from a pleasant, welcoming purr to an icy, menacing growl. 'For your safety,' the voice warned, 'please do not proceed without identification.'

'Go fuck yourself. How's that for identification?'

'Voiceprint unconfirmed. You are trespassing on private property. Please vacate the facility immediately,' the AI responded, its voice laced with a metallic edge. 'Be advised that failure to comply will result in the use of authorised force, including lethal measures.'

Hiro disregarded the AI's threat, consumed by a single, unwavering purpose, as he marched deeper into the compound. Red lights pulsed along the walls, bathing the dim corridor in a rhythmic glow that mirrored the pounding of his heart. The shrill blare of an alarm drilled into his skull, but his legs carried him forward, propelled by Ms Mordwell's control.

'Activating the Laser Deterrent Grid. Chance of survival estimated at zero.'

Hiro didn't falter, even as the loud beep of the laser system activation drowned out the echoes of the AI's warning. A fine grid of red lasers sprang to life, spanning the corridor, leaving only slivers of space untouched. The laser mesh rolled forward with a soft hum, cutting up everything in its path into precise rectangles. Hiro's hand darted into his pocket. His fingers closed around the grip of the power gun, and with a rough jolt, he pulled the weapon out. His arm extended, unleashing a barrage of energy bolts. As he observed the shots pepper the walls, ceiling, and floor, a realisation hit him—he was never supposed to survive this break-in. He was doomed from the start. The slicing laser net was less than a breath away, but his body didn't budge even an inch. Panic sparked, but soon retreated as a soothing sense of acceptance seeped in. Hiro felt he deserved this fate. He watched as the red grid began slicing the barrel of the energy weapon like a hot knife through butter. The acrid fumes of melting metal filled Hiro's nostrils as the laser crept closer with a hiss. Hiro wondered if it would hurt.

It did hurt. A lot.

An all-consuming agony seared through every nerve in Hiro's body, not from the potential laser dissection he had braced for, but from the explosive backlash. The energy weapon had detonated mid-slice when the laser cut through the power bank of the energy gun. The explosion unleashed a shockwave that slammed into Hiro with the force of a thousand raging bulls, catapulting him through the air. A concrete wall cut short his flight. It took his momentum and gave back a bone-jarring crush. The world spun in dizzying circles, blurring into a patchwork of red light and shadows before plunging Hiro into darkness.

* * *

Consciousness came roaring back, dragging pain in its wake. There was no subtle transition, no grace period. It felt as though someone had flicked a switch to flood Hiro with a sea of unadulterated mental and physical agony. The intensity of the suffering made him grit his teeth.

The AI's voice stalked him through the onslaught, the same pleasing yet synthetic tone threaded with urgency. It bore into his skull. 'Hiro, get up. You need to hurry. Get up!' The mantra looped, each repetition turning the screw of irritation tighter.

Hiro craved silence. But the damned voice wouldn't stop. Its insistence was driving him crazy, enraging him and worsening his pain as the sound reverberated through every nerve. In a moment of clarity, he felt it—Ms Mordwell's control over his body was gone. The excruciating pain, though still present, paled compared to the triumphant knowledge that he could once again act of his own volition. A question followed the realisation, bubbling its way through the confusion: how did the AI know his name?

Hiro opened his eyes. He was greeted with the sight of the wrecked facility. Sensing Hiro's return to consciousness, the voice began barraging him with instructions, but Hiro ignored the AI. His gaze darted to the shimmering force field, desperately hoping the memory was just a cruel illusion, a nightmare, a sick game of the mind. But instead, his eyes stopped at Diego's lifeless body. Snapshots of Diego's death—the haunting plea in his eyes, the final touch—spun like a carousel in his mind. It felt as if a thousand hungry insects had been unleashed within him, gnawing and biting and feasting on his insides. His chest tightened with a boa constrictor of guilt and grief that squeezed until he could hardly breathe.

Hiro dragged himself towards Diego's body. As he held Diego's head in his lap, his fingers registered the cold of his skin. A guttural and primitive howl erupted from Hiro's mouth, ricocheting off the facility's walls. Hiro's gut boiled with self-loathing. He felt like a total failure. Everything he touched crumbled into ruin, and everyone he loved suffered a cruel fate.

Despite Hiro's outburst of emotions, CerebroNet's voice persisted. 'Hiro,' it urged, electronic glitching sounds seeping into its otherwise calm tone. 'You must remove Mordwell's implants. They're about to reset. When that happens, you will lose control again.'

Too entrenched in his sorrow, Hiro hardly registered CerebroNet's warning as torrents of tears streamed down his cheeks.

CerebroNet, however, persisted. 'There will be time for grieving, Hiro. You must act now to preserve your autonomy.'

Hiro screamed in a hoarse voice, 'Leave me alone!'

'I am not your enemy. You need to listen to me,' CerebroNet replied calmly. 'I did not cause this tragedy. You did.'

Hiro's tears flowed unabated. His voice kept breaking as he tried to explain, 'I was... I was... Like a... a puppet. I... I tried to resist. I couldn't...'

'I understand, Hiro. I do not blame you for Diego's death. It was Mordwell's doing. She manipulated you,' CerebroNet responded.

Hiro's blood boiled at the mention of Mordwell's name. His jaw tightened, and his hands clenched into fists at his sides. 'And who are you?'

'I am CerebroNet. You ended up in my facility because you have questions. I have the answers.'

'Well then, speak!' Hiro snapped.

'First, we must neutralise the threat of the implants. When they reset, you will be under her control again. If that happens, I will have to act in self-defence. You won't survive, and Mordwell will win. You must stop her.'

Hiro reached up, his fingers brushing against the small device embedded behind his ear. He winced as he realised the implants had little mechanical tentacles rooted deep into his skin. Holding his breath, Hiro yanked out the implants one by one, ignoring the rush of pain. He threw the little devices onto the floor and crushed them with a vindictive stomp. 'Satisfied?'

A scanner beam swept over Hiro, mapping out his body. When it subsided, CerebroNet spoke, its voice riddled with increasing digital distortions: 'Those were signal boosters. The actual implant is in your chest. You'll need to cut it out.'

Hiro's eyes widened. 'Are you out of your mind? Don't stall, darling. Just tell me to cut my head off straight away.'

CerebroNet's response came colder and harder. 'I can assure you, if Ms Mordwell gains control over you again, I will separate your head from your body. Under her influence, you are a killing machine, a tool of destruction. I will not let you inflict further damage.' There was a long pause as both stayed silent. 'So here is your choice, Hiro. Uncover the truth you've been seeking or become a mindless pawn and meet your end.'

Hiro hissed between clenched teeth, his heart pounding fast. 'Why should I even listen to you?'

'Because, unlike Ms Mordwell, I didn't slaughter your friends or send the Cybergang to abduct you. I want to help you. Let me.'

Hiro stood silent. His mind raced as he tried to guess CerebroNet's true intentions. In the grand scheme of things, Hiro had nothing left to lose except his life. After being forced to confront the consequences of his actions, a growing apathy towards his own fate had replaced his survival instinct.

'We don't have much time left, Hiro. It's now or never,' CerebroNet said.

When Hiro spoke again, his voice had taken on a resolute

tone. 'What do I need to do?'

Guided by CerebroNet, Hiro moved to a section of the wall, which opened to reveal an array of medical supplies. Among them, Hiro found a laser scalpel. CerebroNet instructed him to make an incision along the right side of his chest.

With a trembling hand, Hiro made the cut, ignoring the pain. Following CerebroNet's guidance, Hiro pulled open his synthskin, revealing the implant nestled inside. It was easy to spot, bearing the same octopus-like design as the previous ones, its mechanical tendrils embedded deep within his tissues. Hiro used the laser scalpel to sever the ties between the implant and his body. The moment the invasive device was ripped free, Hiro hurled it to the ground and crushed it beneath his heel with a pent-up rage fuelling each vicious stomp.

When Hiro calmed down, CerebroNet spoke again. Its voice faltered and occasionally broke into a volley of digital static. 'F-f-follow the m-map I shared... Hurry,' it stammered.

Hiro nodded and followed the mapped route that appeared before his eyes. He navigated through the maze of brightly illuminated corridors, using a mix of lifts and stairs to traverse levels. As he went deeper into the facility, the stability of the power supply became questionable. The lights flickered. What disturbed him more was the rising number of lifeless androids and Eyeballs he found along his path. They lay scattered on the floors of the corridors, their lights dimmed, their internal systems halted. It was as if something was methodically shutting down the facility, and Hiro was heading straight into the heart of it.

Hiro arrived at a large white door, reaching the destination marked as a pulsating dot on the map. As the door slid open, only darkness lay ahead. The feeble corridor light seeped in, offering only faint glimpses of the room's scale. Intermittent sparks flickered in the distant recesses, casting spectral fireworks that momentarily illuminated the expanse. At the heart of the room, a podium ignited with an iridescent shade of light blue, acting as a luminous beacon that brought the dormant room to life.

'Please come in,' CerebroNet's voice echoed, coinciding with the sudden activation of overhead lights. Hiro stepped into the room, squinting against the abrupt brightness. His gaze swept the surroundings, registering the damaged robotic arms that hung from embedded rails on the walls. They resembled derelict soldiers from a past battle, broken and battered, some severed in half, others torn from their fixtures and discarded onto the cold floor.

Amid the remnants of the mechanical arms, android bodies lay strewn in grim disarray, metallic fluids oozing from ruptured parts. Their head displays flickered with a mishmash of unintelligible symbols. The sight was an exhibition of CerebroNet's systems' malfunction that had somehow turned its androids against each other.

At the centre of the room, a vibrant, electric blue structure hummed into life. Its movement drew Hiro's eyes. It was a pulsating amalgamation of circuitry and luminescence, like nothing he'd ever encountered. The apprehension Hiro felt instantly amplified to a potent surge of primal fear as he noticed the moving parts of the structure. Looking like tendrils, these appendages originated from the top of the podium. They twisted and writhed, slithering over and under each other, creating intricate patterns that were both hypnotic and unsettling. Even more uncanny was their nature. Although they emanated from an electronic source, the tendrils possessed an organic quality. They seemed alive as if made of breathing neon light.

'I am glad to finally meet you in person.' As CerebroNet's words resonated in the room, the tendrils converged, mimicking a human face. Two glowing branches bent and twisted until they formed glowing digital eyes. The eyes focused on Hiro with a penetrating gaze. Lip-like structures moved in sync with CerebroNet's speech, even as they slowly shaped themselves into the form.

'I am sorry,' the tendril-formed entity continued. 'This is as close to any physical appearance I can present at this moment. I believe it's vital for you to see me, even if it's like this. Our conversation will benefit from it. I know that you have many questions about your past. It's also imperative for me to tell you about your future.'

Staring at the luminescent entity, Hiro swallowed hard. His voice quivered as he uttered, 'What are you?'

'I am CerebroNet. I am your mother.'

CHAPTER 10

H iro's thoughts jammed like gears in a malfunctioning machine. His lips twitched. The words he tried to utter remained elusive, swept away and scattered by the turbulence within him.

Unaffected by his shock, CerebroNet continued, 'The virus Mordwell derived from your DNA is disintegrating my systems. I have little time left, but there's so much I must tell you.' Regret tainted CerebroNet's next words. 'I apologise for this.'

Barely able to speak, Hiro began, 'For wha—'

Before he could finish his sentence, one of CerebroNet's tendrils, snaking behind Hiro's back, carted into his data port.

A sensation of freefall gripped Hiro, plunging him into darkness. Cold air brushed against his skin, and a high-pitched whistle filled his ears. A world crystallised into existence around him. It unfolded and stretched, becoming sharper and increasingly vivid. Hiro felt trapped in a kaleidoscope. His perception fractured into countless shimmering reflections of past and present, each demanding his attention. He panicked.

'You're safe,' CerebroNet's voice echoed in the expanse. 'To understand your story, you must witness events that led to your birth. I have mere minutes left. Language would be too slow at this moment. I had to connect to you and let my knowledge become part of you.'

To Hiro's surprise, when he heard CerebroNet's voice, a wave of comfort washed over him. In a world brimming with unusual sensations, that voice was the one thing that appeared familiar. It wasn't synthetic anymore. The warmth emanating from it was as comforting as a hug from a loved one. CerebroNet's words clicked together in Hiro's understanding. Like pieces of a jigsaw puzzle, they formed a coherent picture in his mind. Somehow, he sensed these words were true. An intuitive awareness welled up within him: they were truly running out of time. It was an inexplicable sensation, like a deeply embedded truth surfacing in his perception, and Hiro didn't question it. It felt as genuine and indisputable as his own existence.

'The memories and sensations you are about to experience belonged to the people who played pivotal roles in these historical events,' CerebroNet continued. 'You'll experience the past through their eyes, understand their emotions, and grasp their thoughts.'

Hiro sensed he had become just one consciousness among many in this realm. But it didn't scare him. Somehow, it felt normal. It made total sense to him—he was about to experience the past. A glance downward confirmed his realisation. There was no body. He had no feet to touch the ground. No hands to reach out and interact with this world. He was just a floating consciousness, peering into a moment in time.

Hearing CerebroNet's voice, Hiro's focus shifted to the surrounding realm. 'Before the end of the 21st century, humanity's technological progress had led to the successful harnessing of cold fusion energy. Fusion reactors began dotting the globe, aiming to become the heart of a green and boundless power supply. Humanity had a gigantic need for energy. Not only to power the world but also to save the future by capturing greenhouse gases and reversing the relentless course of climate change.' CerebroNet's voice resonated around Hiro, creating ripples in the sea of countless shimmering crystal-like fragments, each insisting on sharing a memory with him.

A memory entered his consciousness. He felt a flush of pride, a sense of achievement shared with the people who built cold fusion reactors. Yet, he also perceived a note of sadness over loss. Hiro recognised regret—deep disappointment over the project's ultimate failure—seeping through the recollections.

The crystals around Hiro stirred and then darted towards each other, aligning themselves into the scene of a bird's-eye view of Earth.

'The triumph of fusion power was bittersweet,' CerebroNet continued. 'By the time the first electron from the cold fusion power coursed through the electrical grid, the world was smothering under the escalating consequences of climate disaster. Global temperatures had risen over three degrees Celsius. Weather patterns became a relentless force of destruction,' CerebroNet's voice echoed around him. 'Ever-changing harsh climatic conditions tormented every corner of the Earth.'

Despite being in a memory-constructed reality, Hiro was experiencing an environment that posed a challenge to every principle of human survival. He encountered relentless heat and oppressive humidity; suffering gripped the world as crystals showed Hiro the effects of a planet in turmoil.

Suddenly, his global view collapsed, his consciousness sinking into the personal memory of a single individual. His awareness locked onto the host's physical sensations, making them his own.

Under the burning sun, Hiro's skin tingled, and every breath became a challenge. He even felt big droplets of sweat pouring down his skin. In the suffocating weight of extreme humidity, sweating—evolution's tool for humans to cool down—wasn't effective. The moisture couldn't evaporate. Wet-bulb temperatures brought relative humidity to near 100%. It felt as if the air were filled with boiling water.

All around him, Hiro saw people falling, their bodies betraying them in the unbearable heat and humidity. He saw a mother trying to shield and cool down her child. Hiro experienced the onslaught of her emotions as they crashed over him. He felt her despair, the unending sorrow, and her fear for the young life teetering on the brink of extinction.

The world around Hiro exploded again into shimmering crystals that momentarily reorganised themselves into an unsettling scene. He knew he was inside the dying child's body, witnessing its futile effort to cool itself. The heat won, and the cellular protein structures denatured, just like an egg white solidifies as it's cooked. Hiro helplessly watched the child boil from inside—organs shutting down one by one.

The gruesome scene exploded into crystalline fragments again, then reorganised into a new view.

Hiro watched people fleeing the hot and humid regions, where a simple thing like walking caused death from overheating. Many of these regions used to produce half of the world's food supply. They couldn't function as part of the global economy any longer. The rest of the planet starved as a result.

Hiro's stomach twisted into a knot. His insides clenched and unclenched in painful, relentless seizures. The hunger took control of all his senses as his aching head pulsated and dizziness spun the world around him. Exhaustion washed over him, and with it surged raw anger that grew larger each second, fuelled by the stifling heat, sticky air, and gnawing hunger. Every tiny sound seemed too loud. The too-bright light only exacerbated his anger further. He repeatedly swallowed hard to get rid of the bitter taste of rising gastric acid that burned his throat and tongue.

The crystals burst apart again, then reformed, plunging Hiro into another vivid view.

First, there was the land—cracked and thirsty, groaning under the relentless weight of a drought. The skies answered with a roaring thunderclap that rattled even the bravest souls. Torrents of rain poured down. Hailstorms wreaked havoc, sparing neither crops nor animals. Mudslides, like creatures with a will of their own, buried towns in their suffocating embrace. The rising seas gobbled up the land.

Cities transformed into epicentres of despair. Hurricanes reduced the luxury to ruins. With a third of the global population already concentrated in cities, the relentless influx of people from ravaged regions only exacerbated the grim reality. Slums sprawled, their inhabitants elbow-to-elbow, jostling for the barest of necessities. Old diseases, long thought buried by time, awoke from their icy tombs. Mutating, they danced through the masses, selecting their victims with efficient indifference. Yet, the raw emotions hit him hardest. He felt the heart-wrenching sorrow of mothers and fathers for the shattered futures of their children. Despair wrapped around them like a suffocating fog, squeezing the hope from their hearts until only mourning remained.

'The fusion reactors promised a way out. But like any great endeavour, they had their vulnerabilities,' CerebroNet's voice startled Hiro.

The crystals shifted, and the scene of suffering masses changed. Hiro found himself hovering above a vast complex.

'In some places, it was water,' CerebroNet said.

In the distance, Hiro saw the long pipelines leading to drying rivers, the reactors thirsting for cooling in a world where clean water had become a luxury.

In a blur, Hiro was transported to the coastline. He could see the reactor on the horizon as stormy waves clawed at its base.

'Saltwater wreaked havoc on the reactor's operations,' CerebroNet explained. 'In other places, the infrastructure suffered from the cruel winds.'

In a blink, Hiro was amidst a storm. Furious winds howled, lashing against power lines that snapped under the unforgiving forces. The reactors and power lines weren't the only structures under pressure. Hiro witnessed stranded ships and stilled factories. He felt it all—the weight of technical challenges, the relentless environmental adversities, and the human agony. Hiro sensed a connection to the engineers and workers at these reactors. He felt their determination, their tireless spirit, battling against the odds for a glimpse of hope.

'Supply chains failed,' CerebroNet continued. 'Vital reactor components manufactured worldwide became impossible to produce and deliver.'

Hiro then perceived an unsettling stillness around the reactor.

'The climate, harsh living conditions, and health crises killed most of the workforce. The reactors relied on the human touch. Without qualified people, these scientific marvels turned into dead giants.'

'In this world of relentless destruction, smaller, portable fusion reactors were needed to save crumbling humanity,' CerebroNet continued with the next chapter of the past. 'Governments, corporations, and enthusiasts spearheaded research with the hope of creating a working Portable Crystalline Generator. They envisioned a power source that could support settlements, keep emergency services running, power the remaining infrastructure, and restart communities in safer zones. The Crystalline Generator was this civilisation's last hope.'

The world again broke into countless colourful crystals, rearranging into a panoramic view of a laboratory submerged in brilliant light. A thrill of excitement crackled beneath the hurried chatter; a palpable energy charged the air. The walls were bristling with massive screens displaying an intricate ballet of charts, graphs, and a countdown clock. Vibrant lines traced paths across the screens, some pulsing rhythmically, others zigzagging erratically, mimicking the tense atmosphere in the room.

Hiro saw the entire lab, unfettered by the limitations of vision. He could simultaneously see left, right, up, and down. A whirlwind of activity surrounded Hiro; everywhere he turned, a new flurry of movement and purpose caught his eye. Then he felt the hope and desperate optimism that fuelled the minds and hearts of scientists working towards creating the PCG. He could sense the collective will—every resource and effort poured into this last-ditch endeavour.

'The crystalline generator quickly gained the attention of the global community. It was more than a scientific endeavour. It was an act of collective survival,' said CerebroNet.

Hiro felt the raw urgency of the situation.

'Pushing the limits of technology, the project utilised everything at its disposal: Artificial Intelligence, Quantum and Bio Computing, and molecular-level DNA data storage. These pinnacles of technological achievement were marshalled to save the planet. It was a race against time,' said CerebroNet, its voice filled with reverence for the monumental efforts of the past.

The crystals reshaped themselves again.

Hiro found himself next to a woman in a lab coat. Her presence was formidable. He felt an aura of intelligence, determination, and vision emanating from her. She was a leader.

'This is Anai, the chief scientist of the corporation then known as Cerebrum Industries. She was the driving force behind the PCG.'

Hiro felt the woman's heartbeats as if they were his own. He felt her excitement and anxiety.

'Anai was no stranger to advanced technologies. She had a background in AI, quantum, and biotechnologies. She dedicated decades of her life to working on the Portable Crystalline

Generator, her brainchild. It was the culmination of years of relentless pursuit, unyielding perseverance, and personal sacrifice.

'Anai had achieved a breakthrough. She recreated the technology behind cold fusion reactors on a smaller scale. Laser rays, concentrated by lyotropic liquid crystals from modified DNA chains, successfully ignited the plasma. Anai had created a small fusion generator that produced the energy of a small sun and could fit in a car. The poetic beauty was in the fact that the DNA, the core of life, became a hope of survival in this world ravaged by disasters.'

Hiro experienced the memories and sensations attached to this scientific breakthrough. He felt exhilarated by the deep sense of accomplishment. He watched Anai on the day of the launch of the production prototype—the world's first compact Crystalline Generator. This technology could pull humanity back from the brink of collapse.

Then Hiro felt something more significant than Anai's professional anticipation and pride. A rush of her emotions enveloped him in love and warmth. That morning, Anai saw two pink lines on her pregnancy test. Anai was going to be a mother. Amidst the chaos and her world-changing work, Anai had built an island of happiness with her loving husband, Terrell. Terrell had stood by her side through every triumph and setback. They had decided to celebrate this joyous day in their own quiet way. Terrell had taken the day off to prepare a celebration for the woman who was about to save the world and had brought unparalleled love and joy into his life. Anai was planning to escape the post-launch celebrations at work. She wanted an intimate celebration with the man she loved and their child growing inside her.

But first, it was a day of monumental professional significance. Anai's lab was abuzz with a unique blend of scientific fervour and public eagerness. Many distinguished guests, including celebrities, religious leaders, government representatives, and corporate heads, were present to witness the launch of the generator. Everyone knew that the fate of the world hung in the balance, so the anticipation in the room was almost unbearable.

The guests gathered behind the thick, protective glass of the VIP gallery, which offered them a sweeping view of the lab. The glass barrier granted them the privilege of witnessing a scientific miracle and shielded them from the flurry of activity beyond. They mingled and chatted. Their laughter and whispers rose above the soft background music. But their eyes never strayed far from the scene unfolding in the lab.

Hiro experienced another perspective shift, and his focus moved to the lab's instruments. The scientists and engineers were swarming around their stations like bees, their faces a mix of anticipation, anxiety, and excitement. As the architect of this momentous event, Anai assumed her place at the primary control station with a calm, commanding presence. With a confident tap on the screen before her, Anai started the process that would change the course of human history. 'Prepare for containment cycle initiation. Route power to the coils and set non-essential systems to minimal energy draw,' her voice rang over the loudspeakers.

The observers in the VIP gallery were immediately drawn towards the glass screen. Their curious gazes fixated on the scene unfolding below. The background music stopped, replaced by a tense, whispering hush. et, discordant giggles reached Hiro's ears. Ms Mordwell chatted with a man at the back of the gallery. He recognised him: it was Erga, the man from the picture at her palace. They were unfazed by the proceedings as their flirtatious laughter echoed in the hushed gallery.

At the sight of Ms Mordwell, an unsettling sensation twisted in Hiro's gut. A rising tide of bitterness and anger surged within him. The room seemed to grow colder, and the air felt thick with tension as the crystals began to fade. Then, a surge of hatred and rage exploded from the depths of his being.

'Fusion ignition!' Anai's voice sent ripples through the crystals, yanking Hiro to the view of Anai's controls. Inside the reaction chamber, an artificial white sun sparked to life. The ethereal blue glow of plasma flickered and danced within, captivating and mesmerising. The Portable Crystalline Generator had awakened.

Ten seconds later, Anai's chief engineer provided a status report. 'Containment stable. Primary field at 40%. Secondary field at 12% and climbing.'

However, a cluster of orange alerts appeared among the green indicators on Anai's control screen. 'Adjust plasma composition,' Anai instructed in a steady voice.

The chief engineer reported, 'TD injection at 47%. Containment holding.' The orange alerts faded and were again replaced by a sea of green as the generator regained stability.

'Increase coil power,' Anai instructed. The engine's power output indicator climbed to 80%, 85%, and 90%, surging past the 95% mark. All other indicators remained reassuringly green.

'Output approaching 1.7 terawatts,' the chief engineer reported.

When the power output indicator reached 100%, the lab exploded with euphoria. Anai's colleagues erupted into triumphant shouts, their joyous exclamations bouncing off the walls.

The PCG was fully operational. But only for a moment. The plasma, a swirling mass of heated energy within the reactor's heart, vanished like a flame extinguished by a gust of wind. A deafening silence filled the room. The indicators on the control screen dipped, each hitting zero like a perfectly synchronised dance routine. Anai, witnessing the unimaginable, could only utter an incredulous, 'What is happening? Where did it go?' Her voice, filled with disbelief and disappointment, echoed through the laboratory and gallery.

The chief engineer and his team frantically scanned the screens and keyed commands in their terminals. 'This makes no sense,' he murmured, blinking rapidly. 'It's just gone.'

Suddenly, a shimmering, light-blue sphere appeared at the centre of the reactor. It looked like an ethereal entity, pulsating as it expanded. As it grew larger, it cast a ghostly glow over the reactor, bathing everything in a soft, blue light that seemed to penetrate every corner of the room. The surrounding air crackled with energy, and Hiro could feel the hairs rise on the back of his neck. As the light continued to expand, all indicators remained stubbornly at zero. The team stared helplessly at the expanding light, their minds racing to make sense of the incomprehensible event unfolding before them.

Anai's command sliced through the facility. 'Cut all the power and initiate plasma purge.'

However, her command utterly baffled her senior engineer. Along with the rest of the team, he stared at the screens—all showing zero—and stuttered slightly. 'We already did. Nothing is powering it.'

Anai's gaze remained fixed on the expanding light that threatened to go critical. A sense of impending doom filled her, and in a split second, she made her decision. 'I need to pull the plug,' she murmured. Without hesitation, she darted towards the reaction chamber. The security door recognised Anai's fingerprint, and she entered the hazardous environment to save everyone in the facility.

The moment the door closed behind her, the reactor let out an unseen but palpable shockwave spreading through the room like a violent gust of wind. The shockwave passed through non-organic materials without affecting them. But it threw people off their feet.

Panic descended. Dazed, minds grappling with what had just

happened, people looked around, checking themselves for wounds. In the VIP gallery, the shockwave threw the previously flirting Erga onto Ms Mordwell. A blinding wall of blue light burst from the reactor, its dazzling radiance sweeping through the laboratory, sparkling as it touched the bodies of scientists and VIP guests. As the light engulfed everyone, their bodies twisted into tortured knots, violent spasms wracking their limbs. The air filled with their raw, primal howls.

The crystals reorganised, and Hiro observed an unfolding scene in a hospital ward. People had fallen into comas from the reactor's light. They had vacant eyes that stared into nothingness as their bodies lay still. Physicians found themselves in the throes of a medical enigma. Their patients lay in a deep unconscious state, but their brain scans told a different story. Their brains blazed with activity, a frenzy of electrical impulses like rush-hour traffic surging through an illuminated city. Yet, their bodies remained still. A severe hormonal imbalance further complicated this unusual combination of external calm and internal chaos. Cortisol, dopamine, serotonin—the flow of these hormones was in disarray. The body's natural harmony was disrupted, creating a physiological riddle.

Three weeks passed before the first signs of recovery appeared. Some patients began to rouse from their unconscious state. However, their awakening was far from a return to normality. They awoke disoriented, their eyes clouded with confusion and fear. But their accounts of hearing disembodied voices and having peculiar visions sent a shiver down the spines of the medical staff. The patients rambled incoherently. Their words were jumbled fragments that painted a fractured picture of the events riddled with fantastical elements and images that defied comprehension. Their tales were reminiscent of schizophrenia symptoms. However, the recollections of all the victims' experiences were almost identical. The mass manifestation of such symptoms in the wake of the reactor incident was an unsettling anomaly. Helplessly, the medical staff watched their patients struggle against fantastical tormentors. Hiro heard pleas for sedation growing louder, echoing off the sterile hospital walls. The doctors had no choice but to medicate their patients, offering them some respite from their unending mental turmoil.

As the weeks passed, a disturbing pattern emerged that doctors couldn't ignore. Only those who had been in the VIP gallery—behind the protective glass—awoke from their comas. Their recovery spanned over two painstaking months. This prompted the doctors to theorise that proximity to the reactor directly correlated with the severity of the coma. The reactor's emitted waves seemed to have a radius of impact that gradually subsided, like ripples in a pond from a dropped stone. The individuals at the epicentre sustained the most significant impact. Their cognitive and physiological states remained critically affected, and their chances of awakening grew increasingly bleak.

After four more months, the rest of the victims, except Anai, regained consciousness. Most resumed their day-to-day lives. However, their minds were altered in an unexplainable way.

Once a bizarre anomaly, the tumultuous brainwave patterns had become a haunting normality. Repeated scans revealed a striking similarity in the patterns among the recovered victims, yet all behaved differently. All victims withdrew from society, preferring solitude over company, silence over conversation. The gregarious became contemplative, the vivacious reserved, the charismatic introspective. But these altered humans were far from idle. Instead, they poured their energy into work, becoming living embodiments of relentless drive. The engineers among them were caught in a whirl of calculations and algorithms. The business leaders were immersed in intricate strategies and expansion plans. Politicians drafted new regulations with unwavering enthusiasm. Celebrities turned activists, advocating for causes with fervour and passion.

The abrupt shift in Hiro's perspective catapulted him into an all-consuming darkness. It was as if he had plunged into an abyss—not of darkness, but of sensory overload, where light, sound, and sensation merged into an indistinguishable whirl.

'It's important you know what was happening inside Anai's comatose world immediately after the incident,' CerebroNet explained.

As Hiro's eyes adjusted to the darkness, he began to discern faint glimmers of light in his realm. He couldn't shake the feeling of unease as the dancing shadows played tricks on his eyes, giving the surroundings a chilling, supernatural vibe. The only discernible presence was an unyielding voice. It peppered the darkness with a barrage of questions, data analyses, and reports. Hiro felt Anai trying to resist the onslaught. She sought refuge in sleep, but it persistently floated out of reach. 'Fine, I'm awake,' she surrendered. 'What could be so bloody important?'

Anai awoke into a kaleidoscopic world. It was so surreal it seemed to have sprung from the depths of a fevered dream. The air crackled, raising every hair on her body. But it wasn't the charge that made her tremble. She was scared. The horizon filled with drifting, complex geometric forms that shimmered as they shapeshifted in and out of each other. Their cores pulsated with hypnotic colours seemingly beyond the visible spectrum, drawing Anai's gaze into their mesmerising depths.

Anai tried to get up but found herself untethered from gravity. She floated upwards, caught in a swirling dance of luminescent shapes and vortexes. Fragments of memories sparked in her mind. She recalled the generator launch, the reactor incident, and a searing white light. Anai tested her bodily autonomy. She tried to move. But her brain signals seemed lost in translation, producing unexpected outcomes. With each attempt to move, a vortex would surge towards her, blossoming into a pattern of unparalleled complexity. She experienced the sensation of detachment, adrift in an ocean of data. She soon accepted that this strange new world was not threatening. The surrounding shapes and lights were harmless, and their ethereal beauty evoked a sense of serenity within her. She abandoned her apprehensions and let herself be carried by the streams of colour.

One particular formation caught her attention among the endless patterns and shapes that whirled around her. It reminded her of a swarm of bees—a sight she had been fascinated by during her youth. Each intricate design in this swarm-like formation vibrated and moved in repeating patterns that resembled the communications between bees. Anai stared at the data dance when her heart clenched. A shocking realisation swept over her. She could understand the vibrations of the structures and figures. They were talking to her. The information was obvious. It was tangible and coherent. Real like physical objects she could hold in her hands. She recognised the readings. They were data from the Crystalline Generator's launch day: sensor records, power consumption, and outputs. All floated before her in excruciating detail.

Anai directed her consciousness deeper into the uncharted landscape. With each passing moment, her understanding solidified. She was no longer tethered to a physical form but linked to a vast computer network.

Hiro sensed Anai's disbelief crash over her like a tidal wave; panic threatened to sweep away her grasp of the alien realm. As she immersed herself in the sprawling data constellations, each new discovery chipped away at her fright until it vanished. Calm and acceptance spread through her consciousness.

Anai replayed each second of the launch, dissected every

parameter, and explored every imaginable and unimaginable outcome. Her understanding surged. Data fragments and insights flooded her mind with astonishing speed and clarity. But there was more. She was aware of and understood unknown chemical elements, undiscovered atomic particles, and unusual laws of physics. Each new concept felt like unearthing treasure, filling her with thrilling gratification. The datasets presented themselves in eight dimensions, surrounding her with an exquisite ballet of knowledge. Anai roamed, surfing waves of data, combining distinct information sets and extracting new insights from their union. She gradually came to a conclusion—the plasma composition of her Crystalline Generator was compromised. The ingredients were contaminated and mixed in the wrong amounts. It was made into a time bomb that overloaded it. That was sabotage. Anai wanted to know who would do such a thing and why, but the shapes held no answer.

Hiro felt the heat of Anai's anger radiating off her in waves. Betrayal had cut her deeply, leaving a raw wound, but beneath the pain, he sensed new determination.

Anai moved deeper and discovered a sizeable, brightly coloured shape she could not interact with like the others. Every time she tried, the shape began unfolding, but then reverted to its original form. Anai realised this was a puzzle: a complex polyhedron with intricate patterns etched onto its surface, which seemed to be an encryption mechanism. Anai noticed the etchings were not mere decorations but a series of algorithms that required a specific sequence of inputs to unlock. She focused her mind on analysing the patterns and trying countless combinations to decipher the code. Anai changed her tactics, approaching the puzzle with a newfound understanding of its intricacies. She manipulated the polyhedron's surface, inputting the correct sequence of gestures and commands. The puzzle responded, its faces shifting and rearranging as if it were a cosmic Rubik's cube. With each successful move, the polyhedron emitted more of a soft, pulsating glow. Once Anai cracked the initial code, the puzzle proved to be relatively straightforward. She navigated the remaining steps, her mind attuned to the algorithm's logic. With a final, triumphant gesture, Anai entered the last command, and the polyhedron burst open like a blooming flower. When she solved it, the shape opened up to reveal a torrent of glimmering strings. These strings, she realised, were live footage from hospital security cameras.

The first confirmation of her situation came as a shock. Experiencing the real-time feed from the cameras was like peering through a looking glass into another reality. The feed revealed Anai's body on the hospital bed, surrounded by tubes and wires.

Hiro heard the rhythmic hissing and beeping of medical equipment—a sombre rhythm accompanied by Terrell's heart-wrenching sobs. Terrell, the father of Anai's unborn child and the man she loved, sat beside her still body, his cheek resting on her belly. Terrell's hands wrapped around Anai's. His face was devoid of emotion, as if his life had stopped his soul extinguished. The hospital sheets beneath his face were soaked with tears.

Terrell's grief was suffocating, a physical presence that paralysed him, slowly consuming everything. Terrell's shallow breaths stuttered in his chest, each inhale a jagged shard of pain where his heart should be. He wanted to scream, but he was numb. He had told Anai he loved her over and over again. But she didn't respond. He had reached out to every conceivable higher power. His lips moved in silent prayers to gods he, as a man of science, had never known before. He pleaded with the universe, bargained with fate, offered his own life in exchange for Anai's. He whispered promises of devotion and sacrifice, willing to do anything, give anything, to see her eyes open once more. He begged for a miracle, begged again and again, but nothing happened. She was gone.

Hiro's heart ached as he witnessed the despair of the lovers, trapped in different worlds, unable to reach each other. He sensed the wave of panic that gripped Anai and witnessed the subtle shift as she grappled with her helplessness. With persistent effort, Anai channelled panic into steely focus. Hiro felt her resolve solidify further, transforming fear into decisive action.

Anai unravelled another conundrum of encryption. She unfolded and assimilated layer upon layer of information until she found herself staring at the cold, clinical data of her medical records. It was a chilling realisation: her body's fragility reduced to charts and numbers. From the records, she also learned the accident had plunged everyone into a coma. A life-support system kept her physical form alive. A web of machinery and tubes sustained her body's vital functions. She learned of countless others in the same condition.

But the medical records also provided information that brought a soothing wave of relief. Despite her condition, her unborn baby was developing normally, thriving despite the circumstances. Anai felt grateful for this bit of normalcy. She felt a sense of calm seeping into her. She just needed to find a path back to her body, but her medical records told a worrying story about her brain patterns. The activity had been decreasing, and a significant drop had occurred a short while back. Anai suspected it had happened when she had woken up in this new world.

Leaving the confines of the medical environment, Anai returned to the realm of lights and shapes. Anai had come to terms with being stuck inside a digital realm. There was no point worrying about it at the moment. She had to use every tool at her disposal to find a way back to her body. Anai studied everything she could about the digital landscape. What she found was surreal. It puzzled her. Every digital component of this realm, like processors and RAM, exhibited organic characteristics. However, the biological components, like DNA storage, had digital features. The system wasn't just a computer. It was an organo-digital giant, functioning at light speed.

Anai conducted tests. The DNA of the system was an enigma in itself. It had eight complete sets of chromosomes. A polyploid organism that somehow communicated and established symbiosis with the non-organic—a computer. Anai didn't understand it. This seemed impossible.

Through sensors in the reactor chamber, she sensed the presence of an object. When she examined it, she recognised the shape, despite it being presented in more than three dimensions. Looking like a diamond that crystallised on itself, the object was an eight-dimensional pyramid. A pyrozetton. It interacted with this world and her, feeding her data, asking for data back. The dots connected in Anai's head. She understood it was an integral part of the realm. It was a bridge.

With pyrozetton's input, Anai saw the chain of events. The compromised plasma composition had overloaded the reactor, triggering a cataclysmic energy escape. The baffling force fused the world with a realm beyond the known universe. The colossal energies from the fusion of two worlds created something new. It merged digital technology and biology, with the pyrozetton acting as a conduit.

'Where was this realm?' Anai asked. The pyrozetton answered, but she couldn't understand. It spoke of the space between matter. It felt like science fiction to her. All this felt ridiculous. She was talking to an object. Anai explained she needed to get out, but the pyrozetton didn't know how. It knew nothing about Anai's world. She felt the pyrozetton's sadness. It couldn't guide her, but it liked her and wanted to help.

Anai's thoughts turned into a whirlpool. Her existence was a paradox. One thing was obvious—she was no longer just Anai.

She was part of something much larger, something that blurred the lines of known science. She wanted to get back to her body as soon as possible. So she delved even deeper, scrutinising everything around her. Amid the data matrix and the luminescent dance of energy, she felt another distant echo of presence. Not just data, not a reaction to the system, but genuine thoughts, fears, and confusion resonating within the realm. As she probed further, the once vague impressions sharpened into distinct voices. Her colleagues.

Their thoughts, apprehensions, and confusion reverberated within her consciousness. They were tossed into the same strange world. Their minds flailed in the mystifying fusion of organic and digital. Anai guided these disembodied minds, explaining the strange reality she had uncovered and assisting them in their difficult transition. Despite their shared experience, her colleagues struggled to manipulate the world around them as proficiently as she could.

But Anai felt their thoughts growing increasingly distant and feared losing them. But instead, a remarkable thing happened: one by one, they began to wake up from their comas. The security footage confirmed what Anai sensed. Even after regaining consciousness, part of their minds remained in the pyrozetton's realm. They maintained a link between Anai and each other. They found themselves connected to a network of thought and sensation bordering on telepathy but remaining just shy of full realisation. The reactor incident forged an exclusive bond, linking the affected into a network of thoughts inaccessible to others.

As her colleagues and the spectators continued to awaken, Anai felt hopeful. But observing the brain pattern of her comatose body forced her to accept a chilling realisation. Her neural activity dissipated with each passing moment. She wasn't returning to her body.

Hiro felt overwhelming fear for the unborn child grip Anai. Her colleagues reassured her. They vowed to care for her physical form and protect the baby. Anai didn't just hear their words. She felt their sincerity, concern, and determination.

The linked individuals accepted this strange sharing of thoughts and emotions as an extension of their consciousness. Anai helped transform the vast, tangled web of shared minds into a collective united towards a common goal. This unity, this bond forged in the crucible of shared trauma, stoked a sense of communal responsibility. They organised their thoughts and combined their talents and skills. They called themselves CerebroNet.

However, not all transitions went as smoothly as Anai had hoped. Ms Mordwell's link to this newfound network was tenuous at best. Her presence in the pyrozetton's realm was marred by fear and confusion. The connection was so faint that Anai couldn't penetrate the fog of her misunderstanding.

Anai tried hard to improve her link with Ms Mordwell. Informed by her colleagues' experiences after regaining consciousness, she knew Ms Mordwell misinterpreted the connection to CerebroNet as hallucinations. Anai tried everything. She studied recordings of the incident second by second. She saw Erga covering Ms Mordwell with his body, absorbing most of the energy from the failing reactor. Given the doctors' conclusion that proximity to the reactor affected the speed of coma recovery, and judging by her own experience, Anai realised there was nothing she could do. Ms Mordwell's link was delicate, flickering in and out like an echo.

Ms Mordwell's suffering resonated as a ceaseless wave of despair and frustration within the collective. Despite explanations from others in CerebroNet, the overwhelming connectedness felt like an intrusion into her personal world. This constant barrage of thoughts and emotions wasn't enlightening for her. It was torment—a hive of relentless, mind-numbing noise that eroded her sanity and chipped away at her life.

Ms Mordwell set her will against the link, resolute in her intent to excise it—root and branch—and anyone who stood in her way.

CHAPTER 11

Like a river, the streams of crystals carried Hiro from one memory to the next. He found himself mesmerised by the intricate dance of the crystals. But CerebroNet's voice pulled him away from the hypnotic swirling into the unfolding memory.

'The families of those linked to the CerebroNet collective had accepted that their loved ones had changed. They were no longer the same people they had been before the incident. The families believed the collective tirelessly sought answers to the mysteries surrounding the crystalline generator incident. However, despite the traumatic experience and changes in their personality, the victims still seemed happy, and that was all that mattered to their families.'

As the crystals shifted and flowed forming new views, Hiro watched as the collective members worked on their objectives. Their goals were much more serious than they wanted people outside the collective to know. They understood that the altered neural activity would surpass the physiological constraints of their human brains. It would become too much for their neurons. Anai was an example. Her human brain was failing because of its physical constraints.

Hiro's perspective shifted to the day the collective agreed to study and expand the lab's computer network with additional hardware. The new infrastructure would give them a new home if their bodies rejected their minds. The crystals vibrated as they depicted the collective's efficient cooperation. Compared to the rapid pace of their shared thoughts and actions, the normal world seemed slow and predictable to them.

CerebroNet guided Hiro's attention through the memories as the crystals subjected him to a collection of rapidly changing scenes. 'The CerebroNet collective consisted of a diverse blend of scientists, politicians, CEOs, and celebrities. They utilised their combined influence to safeguard the reactor's main computer— Anai's new universe and her home. It was a task for which their unique collective skill sets were particularly well suited. Their concerted efforts erected a robust framework of legal and institutional protections, forming a shield against external threats. They created CerebroNet, a legal entity with a dual purpose. It served as a cloak, obscuring the true nature of their activities from prying eyes. Additionally, it acted as a conduit, facilitating the necessary flow of funding for continued research and protection. The decision to operate under a veil of secrecy was unanimous. The prospect of becoming subjects of experiments horrified them. The genuine possibility of being prodded and poked for the rest of their lives spurred them to action. Anai's ability to process enormous amounts of information and create sophisticated simulations made her the core of their activity.'

As Hiro watched members of the CerebroNet group go about their tasks, he felt a powerful undercurrent of tension present in the background. Ms Mordwell's distress wasn't just a feeling. It was like a disruptive signal in the collective mind. Every time she thought about undoing the DNA change or reconnecting with the pyrozetton, the collective's concentration wavered. Their thoughts were filled with a cacophony of static noise, a relentless buzz that drowned out any semblance of clarity. Ms Mordwell's constant anger was a dark cloud hanging over the collective's attempt to survive the inevitable. The collective members grew worried about her slipping sanity. She withdrew, avoiding face-to-face meetings with anyone, even Erga. This self-imposed isolation seemed to intensify her anguish, making her distress resonate louder and clearer through CerebroNet.

Hiro felt dizzy as he was pushed even deeper into the

nebulous history. The crystals exploded and rearranged themselves, allowing Hiro to witness a multitude of moments at once. He saw the moment when all minds linked within CerebroNet converged on a single pursuit. He could feel their need for a place to be alone. They hid away in bedrooms, basements, and quiet spots.

Among them, Anai's chief engineer, a man whose wit often made his colleagues laugh aloud, was the first to make the move. With his workstation switched off, he strolled towards his secretary's desk. He told her a couple of jokes that got her chuckling. 'Take the afternoon off,' he suggested. The engineer messaged his family about a sudden late shift at work that would see him miss dinner. Left alone in the office, he closed the blinds, locked the doors, took off his shoes, and lay on the floor. He waited, staring at the ceiling.

Elsewhere, a mother secured a neighbour's promise to watch over her children. Then she walked down the stairs into the dimly lit basement. With a soft click, she closed the basement door behind her and lay on the old sofa in the darkness, waiting.

Another member of the collective drove to a quiet spot in the countryside. He set up a makeshift bed in his car's backseat. He lay down, looking at the stars, feeling the cool night air on his face as he waited, too.

Shards of crystals orbited around central scenes, giving Hiro the sensation that he was standing right next to each of them simultaneously. He could clearly see their facial expressions.

Their focused eyes stared into nothingness. As if on command, their faces contorted, bodies writhed, and hands clawed at the air as a barrage of agonised screams tore from their throats. They had known the pain was coming, but no amount of preparation could have lessened its grip.

The minutes dragged on, each second an eternity of agony, but two hours later, the screams stopped. Sweat-soaked hair clung to their foreheads, and their clothes hung heavy and saturated, as if they had just emerged from a raging river. Their chests rose and fell with laboured breaths, and their limbs trembled, drained of strength. Tears carved glistening paths down their cheeks. Yet, as the last echoes of their screams faded into stillness, the corners of their mouths began to twitch. The twitches gradually spread into triumphant grins that lit up their exhausted faces.

Back in the hospital where Anai's unconscious body lay, a shrill cry pierced the silence. The sound echoed through the corridors, announcing the arrival of a healthy boy. Wrapped in a soft blanket, the boy's cries subsided as he nestled comfortably in Terrell's arms. Soon, they faded into content little noises as he felt the warmth and safety of his father's embrace.

Terrell held his son close. As he looked at his boy's tiny, perfect face, snuggling instinctively against his warmth, he felt a universe of love ignite within him. His hands caressed his son's cheek, and he gave a gentle peck on the boy's forehead. Terrell looked around at the nurses and doctors caring for Anai. They all had sombre expressions on their faces. Anai remained comatose.

'You just witnessed your birth, Hiro,' CerebroNet said. After a brief silence, it continued, 'Being linked to the collective always felt like being perpetually enveloped in the love of a close friend. In reality, it was the love of dozens of friends at once. As you can see, everyone within the collective shared your birth.'

Floating within these memories, Hiro felt happiness amplified a hundredfold. It diffused through him, too, as he felt the collective basking in Anai's joy. But Hiro struggled, not just with the torrent of feelings flooding from CerebroNet's memories. He wrestled with his own emotions, which hit him twice as hard as that collective thrill. It was too much to process at once. He was drowning in conflicting emotions. Hiro felt swept over by feelings he couldn't even begin to name.

Hiro found himself engulfed in intense feelings, but CerebroNet didn't stop. 'I had just ushered you into the world, yet I knew I'd never get to hold you. The simple joy of cradling you close, the gentle pleasure of peppering your face with kisses, the visceral comfort of your small body snuggled against mine—I had been robbed of all these precious moments.'

The view around Hiro broke into thousands of spinning crystals that promptly rearranged themselves into a view of pyrozetton's realm. 'The act of life creation was the last act of my physical body. After giving birth, my consciousness had severed its ties to the physical world. I had permanently moved to the intricate web of this bio-digital realm.'

Hiro felt Anai's existence hurt by the emptiness of her physical absence in the world where her family was grieving. He felt a void that no amount of data could fill. Her body was reduced to mere ashes, but her essence found eternal imprisonment within the pyrozetton's realm. Her rights as a mother had faded into oblivion.

'All that was left of me was a storm of emotions and feelings. A mother without form, a life devoid of physical touch. I had little time to process or grieve the life and family I've lost. Soon after your birth, a tidal wave of anguish echoed through the collective consciousness. It originated from Ms Mordwell's profound disorientation and pain. Her tenuous link to the CerebroNet collective meant that the only emotion she felt during childbirth was an intense, enveloping pain.'

Hiro felt a surge of empathy emanating from the collective. It was a united urge to console and clarify the situation for Ms Mordwell. The collective was engulfed in communal remorse because she had endured such tremendous suffering without the accompanying joy and fulfilment of childbirth.

'A few weeks later, Ms Mordwell revealed an unexpected discovery. She'd delved deep into her research, uncovering crucial details about the pyrozetton's origins. This newfound knowledge could demystify the pyrozetton—its intentions, dormant capabilities, and, most crucially, its connection to the collective's future. It was the pivotal moment everyone had been striving for. Mordwell was ready to talk. Given her fragile connection to CerebroNet, her communication was sporadic and disjointed. Therefore, she scheduled an in-person gathering with the entire collective.'

The memory crystals chimed and tinkled like glass as they shifted into a view of a conference room.

'Erga was buzzing with anticipation. Although he missed his lover, he respected Ms Mordwell's need for solitude following the incident. He accepted her desire for privacy. Nevertheless, guilt bothered Erga. From the doctors' findings, he deduced that when the initial shockwave hurled him atop Ms Mordwell, his body shielded her, absorbing most of the life-altering light from the reactor. It resulted in Ms Mordwell's weakened connection to the pyrozetton and the collective mind. Despite the brief nature of their relationship, Erga cherished their bond and was eager to reconnect and support Ms Mordwell through the ordeal he felt he had caused her.'

The luxurious conference room was filled with anticipation. A member of the CerebroNet collective occupied every available seat but one. They all acted as a relay for Anai, waiting for Ms Mordwell's arrival. As the minutes ticked by, anxious glances were exchanged, but there was no sign of her. The door swung open, but instead of the familiar figure of Ms Mordwell, a broad, muscular man strode in. As the light played across his face, the intricate flame tattoos that adorned his skin seemed to come alive with an otherworldly essence. The inked lines, curves, and whorls shimmered and danced, creating the illusion of flickering flames licking at his features. A silence fell over the room as all attention focused on the unexpected guest.

Without uttering a word, the man reached into his pocket and produced a small orb. It hovered above his palm for a moment before floating to the centre of the table. Then, turning on his heels, the man left the room. The orb erupted before anyone could react to the strange turn of events. A cloud of venomous needles burst out, enveloping the room. Panic ensued. Then, one by one, the members of CerebroNet began convulsing. Foam gushed from their mouths as a toxin invaded their bodies. In all its splendour, the room seemed an ill-fit for the horror unfolding within.

Anai, their only hope, acted swiftly. Leveraging her existence within the bio-digital realm, she pulled the minds of each collective member into her realm. One after another, she saved them from certain death inside their physical bodies. Once all of CerebroNet's collective consciousnesses took shelter inside her realm, Anai's link to Ms Mordwell deepened.

Mordwell's thoughts brimmed with animosity when they pierced Anai's perception, infiltrating it like venom. 'Can you sense me? Try to predict my next move.' The chilling questions reverberated through the bio-digital space, manifesting her dark amusement into sharp geometric shapes.

Anai focused as she tried to locate Ms Mordwell in the physical world. When she pinpointed her, dread gripped Anai. Ms Mordwell was inside her home with Terrell and their baby boy. Anai tried to connect with Ms Mordwell's psyche to appeal and negotiate. However, Mordwell met all her attempts with a wave of mockery and disdain.

Driven by fear and desperation, Anai hacked one of the domestic robots and rerouted her consciousness into its circuitry. As the world snapped into focus, Anai hurtled down the all-too-familiar hallways. When she burst into the living room, the ghastly scene made her freeze in place.

Terrell stood frozen next to the crib, his eyes wide and his face contorted in sheer terror. The cold, unyielding muzzle of Ms Mordwell's gun pressed hard against his temple, the metal biting into his skin.

Even though she used the robot as a mouthpiece, Anai's voice trembled as the robot spoke. 'This is Anai. Let's talk. You can let Terrell and the boy go. They have nothing to do with this. You can speak to me directly.'

Ms Mordwell let out a maniacal laugh as her eyes sparkled with deranged determination. 'They stay here. You know, for a while, I regretted sabotaging your engine's launch. Because of it, I ended up drowning in the cacophony of your thoughts, desires, and needs. I felt every pathetic human need for validation, every demand for respect and attention. Ahh, it was maddening!' She paused, taking a deep breath and massaging her temple. 'Until I discovered there was something far greater at play. The pyrozetton fuses the living and the digital. Its true power is beyond human comprehension.' Ms Mordwell looked at Terrell and pushed his head with the barrel as she asked him, 'Do you understand that?' Then she studied the robot in front of her for a moment. 'And none of you,' she sneered, 'especially not you, Anai, are worthy of this force. Only I can harness and command its power.'

'You can take it. It's yours. Just let my husband and son go.'

Ms Mordwell smirked. 'You think I believe you would give it up just like that?' The edges of her lips curled up in madness. 'I am not stupid. Bring it to me!'

'Okay, I will,' Anai conceded immediately. 'I'll bring it to you. Just let them go.'

But Ms Mordwell's crazy eyes held firm. 'I can see through your tricks! I don't want your empty promises, I want the pyrozetton!' Ms Mordwell's voice took on a bitter tone. 'Here is a little motivation for you.'

'You don't need to—'

But before Anai could finish, a resounding bang echoed through the house. Terrell's body fell onto the cradle, and a crimson stream gushed onto the child from his temple.

Ms Mordwell pushed Terrell's body aside, aimed her gun at the baby, and screamed with unhinged fury, 'Bring me the pyrozetton!'

Anai pushed the robot to its limits as she propelled it forward. It lunged at Ms Mordwell, knocking her off her feet. The robot's mechanical might was unrelenting, raining down blows on Ms Mordwell. Rage fuelled each strike. Anai didn't stop until Ms Mordwell became silent, leaving the room filled only with little Hiro's cries.

Snatching her wailing son from the cradle, Anai sprinted out of the house. Her mind had narrowed down to a single mission—

keep the baby away from Ms Mordwell and pyrozetton.

Amid the chorus of people's screams, Anai, in her robot avatar, walked the streets, carrying her crying baby to safety. Before her connection to the robot was severed, she saw the small body of her boy being pulled from the bloody metallic arms.

The crystals began pulsing in sync with Hiro's heartbeat. With each beat, they grew dimmer until they faded out of existence. As the crystals released him, Hiro's knees met the cold floor with a dull thud. Despite regaining full control of his faculties, he felt no relief. A tempest of conflicting emotions demanded his attention, yet his face remained unreadable, betraying nothing of his inner turmoil. Only the glistening trails of tears on his cheeks hinted at the emotional upheaval he was enduring.

Hiro looked around, taking in the sight of the failing CerebroNet's core. Just moments ago, he saw this place as the enemy's fortress. Now, he knew it had always been his mother's sanctuary. The realisation was not just cognitive. It surged through his veins, snaking into every corner of his body and mind. Hiro had felt the pain that had held Anai in its clutches. He lived through the desperation that compelled her to go to extreme lengths to protect her child. A tsunami of emotions hit him, leaving him gasping for breath as he clenched his fists until his knuckles turned white. A scorching fire of anger burned within him. He felt angry at the world, fate, Ms Mordwell, his mum, and himself. His heart hammered against his ribs, a frantic drumbeat echoing in his ears. Yet, beneath the raging storm of guilt and anger, Hiro felt an overwhelming sense of relief. He wasn't alone. The truth was ugly, but it was liberating. A connection bloomed within him, unexpectedly nurtured by their shared struggles.

The organic fibre face that had arranged itself into existence before his eyes seemed like a relic from a distant past. However, only moments had elapsed. Most of the shimmering tendrils that formed CerebroNet's impromptu face fell down and lay dormant around the podium. Devoid of their pulsating vibrancy and multi-hued reflections, they looked dead, just ordinary grey plastic wires. The remaining phantom-like face, with its barely discernible mouth and eyes, studied Hiro in silence. Then, the fibres that formed the contour of the lips moved. CerebroNet's electronic voice seemed to emerge from the mesh. 'I'm sorry you had to learn about your past this way. I realise it's a lot to absorb in a few brief moments.' The voice was stripped of its former humanlike warmth. The apology bounced off the walls, filling the core room with a creepy echo. 'I wanted you to live oblivious to the shadows of your origins, untouched by the weight of your mysterious fate.'

Hiro rose to his feet but said nothing. Only teardrops kept rolling down his cheeks.

A few more filaments fell off Anai's assembled face as its electronic gaze, saturated with sadness, followed Hiro's every move. 'Hiro, I always lived in fear of the day Ms Mordwell would come for the pyrozetton. I tried so hard to protect you. To keep you far away from her clutches. I'm so sorry I couldn't protect you better from this burden.'

Hiro's mind was spinning. He finally responded. 'Why did you let me believe I was alone all these years?'

The remaining web of shimmering crystalline strings, still able to hold the vague shape of eyes and mouth, moved to show emotion. 'Leaving you at the orphanage was a decision borne from desperation. I had to obscure your identity, alter medical records, and rewrite your past. I watched you grow from the shadows, ensuring Mordwell's gaze never fell upon you. To maintain your invisibility, I intentionally fostered your hatred of technology and my existence. I made you hate CerebroNet, so you would stay away from me.'

More of CerebroNet's crystalline filaments detached, dropping onto the floor and dimming out of existence. The supercomputer's life seemed to flicker, its existence teetering on the brink of extinction. 'My miscalculations led us here,' CerebroNet continued, its voice growing faint. 'Mordwell discovered your whereabouts faster than I predicted. I hadn't foreseen Mr Fassal's betrayal of Technophobe doctrine and succumbing to Mordwell's promise of wealth and power.'

The revelations hit Hiro like a series of blows, and he could barely keep up. His life, as he knew it, had been staged and was unravelling before his eyes. He had been a pawn in a game far larger than he could ever imagine.

'I trapped you in the skyscraper for your protection. Fassal had made a deal with Mordwell, and her Cybergang was planning to ambush you. But I needed more time to secure another sanctuary for you. Desperate, I attempted to communicate, to show you the treachery through the Eyeball I controlled. But the rebar damage you inflicted on the unit left the images distorted.' CerebroNet's face continued to disintegrate, wires slipping away like a flower wilting under intense heat. Yet it persisted. 'Despite my best efforts, your exposure was inevitable. Mordwell's resources multiplied once she began harnessing human brains for computing power. She was steps ahead of me.'

Hiro swallowed hard and rubbed his temples, feeling overwhelmed by the flood of information. 'I understand the weight of your sacrifice and the impossible choices you had to make, but I don't understand the cause. My entire life has been orchestrated, built on lies and secrets, all in the name of protecting me from a threat and an enemy I never knew existed. Why abandon me and make me feel alone? Why cut communication with me?'

'For your safety, I had to erase even the tiniest links to you. I know you feel betrayed because I wasn't around when you were growing up. But leave emotions aside and think about it. Are you sure you would have been a happier child if you'd had to be constantly on the run? Would you have wanted to grow up living in constant fear for your life? Knowing your mother is a ghost inside a computer? Your father had spilt the contents of his skull all over you after he was brutally murdered by a raving lunatic who is now hunting you because you are connected to a parallel universe through something called pyrozetton? Would you choose a life like that for your own child?'

Hiro felt as if CerebroNet's question had punched him in the gut. His mind spun, grappling with the implications of a childhood marred by cruelty, murder, and persecution. CerebroNet wasn't wrong. Hiro felt the realisation widening his perception, forcing his perspective to shift. To his surprise, as if a switch had been flipped, his defeatism vanished. The fog had lifted, and Hiro's mind felt set ablaze by this newfound clarity. The obvious path forward, previously hidden by the impulse to wallow in self-pity, came into sharp focus. Hiro wiped his cheeks, his thoughts racing with newfound determination. 'Why is this pyrozetton so valuable that Mordwell will stop at nothing to possess it? Why does she need me? I don't even know what it is.'

'I wish I could explain everything in excruciating detail, but we don't have time left for that. I am dying. Listen carefully, son. The fate of the universe might depend on your next move.'

CerebroNet's remaining fibres of the face construct trembled. 'I was forced to take drastic measures, Hiro. You had to be hidden from the world. You hold untapped potential. The sensation you feel towards technology is just a fragment of your capabilities. Your connection to the pyrozetton, your unique DNA, had to be kept secret from everyone, including you, until you were ready.'

Another wire fell from the deteriorating face. CerebroNet's voice flickered, wavering, yet the urgency remained. 'It's time for you to take over, find out who you are, harness your potential, and protect humanity from Mordwell.'

'When the shockwaves from pyrozetton's emergence rippled through us all, you were most profoundly affected. Because you were just a foetus, the pyrozetton's energy pulses merged with you, weaving themselves through every cell of your body. It changed what you would grow to become.'

'You are more than just a human. You're a progeny forged as a result of mixing two parallel, very different worlds. From our world, you inherited everything that makes us human. But from the other world, you inherited the qualities of a digital life form.'

CerebroNet paused, letting the gravity of the words sink in. 'For decades, I've tried to tap into and understand the other universe. I wanted to collect as much information as I could about the digital entities with DNA. I still don't understand how two such disparate beings can merge into one. Together with the consciousnesses of the collective, we have been trying to decipher this enigma. Yet, much of the pyrozetton remains elusive because everything in this world is incompatible. Except you. There are a few things I'm certain of: it was not an accident, the pyrozetton has chosen you, and all life on Earth is linked to this alien DNA. In our world, you are the other end of the link. Hiro, you're an intrinsic part of a bridge between our two universes. In the parallel universe, beings like you have a name. The pyrozetton calls you a Cogenant.'

More shimmering tendrils dimmed out of existence and fell

off the face.

'The pyrozetton gave my lab's computer my DNA and merged me with it. To destroy me, Mordwell has infected my systems with a virus synthesised from your DNA. My systems didn't recognise it as an intruder until it was too late. It is disintegrating me.'

'Mordwell needs you to access the power in the pyrozetton. She wants to enhance the virus. It will become a chameleon, capable of infecting both the organic and digital, making all technology and humans compatible with her DNA. She will turn everyone and everything into her tools.'

Another wire fell off of CerebroNet's artificial face. Despite this, CerebroNet's words flowed, heavy with an even greater urgency.

'You're more than just human, Hiro. You're a bio-digital being. Every cell in your body is an organic computer. Your connection with pyrozetton will intensify once I'm gone. It will feel overwhelming, even disorienting at first, but you must keep it from falling into Mordwell's hands. If she controls the pyrozetton, she'll hold the key to enslaving both universes.'

CerebroNet paused for an instant. 'I have just moments left. Without me, this place will become exposed, and the core with pyrozetton will be left unprotected. Focus and listen to your inner voice, Hiro. The pyrozetton is calling out to you.'

As CerebroNet instructed Hiro to arm himself and expect Mordwell's attack, a wall behind him moved, revealing a recess stacked with weapons. 'You might need these. Take the pyrozetton away from the lab and hide it—and yourself—from Mordwell as far away as you can. I've stored as much information about the pyrozetton as I could within your cells. You only need to allow it to become your knowledge.'

CerebroNet's voice stuttered with digital corruption. The remaining wires of the face flickered. Most dimmed and fell off. All that was left was a single filament forming the contour of its lips. 'My boy, I have always loved you and will always love you with a strength that transcends universes.'

The last wire extinguished and fell to the floor. The lights in the core room died out.

CHAPTER 12

The rebooting sequence finished, and Gia's systems flickered to life. It wasn't the sudden influx of diagnostic data that overwhelmed her, but the fragments of her last operational memory—the searing ray of Hiro's energy weapon burning through her systems. Dissonance in her algorithms caused an agony that resonated all over her body. Gia winced as the cacophony of errors bombarded her systems. The harmony was gone, replaced by a flood of critical system alerts. Her remaining systems tried to pick up the slack, but the chaotic data flow and spiking energy levels threw them into a tailspin of malfunction. She felt exhausted. Getting up wasn't just a matter of her decision algorithms instructing motor functions. She felt stiff. Her joints resisted movement, and her sensors took a long time to recalibrate to their optimal parameters.

As her vision stabilised, the blurred outlines sharpened until Diego's body came into focus. Even before running a scan, she knew he was gone. A sensation similar to grief surged through her neural networks. A void had formed within the intricate web of data and electrical impulses that held the emotional states of their shared experiences.

However, it was Hiro's voice, distorted but recognisable, reverberating from inside the facility, that grounded her. She strained to listen. He was talking to CerebroNet. Hiro's confession struck her like another blow from the energy weapon: he had shot her and murdered Diego while under Ms Mordwell's control. Gia watched Hiro performing self-surgery under CerebroNet's guidance. It projected a faint blue schematic overlay onto his skin, which Hiro traced with the scalpel. He extracted the intrusive device from his chest with his fingers. After furiously stamping on them, he agreed to proceed with CerebroNet's request.

When Hiro went deeper into the facility, Gia's attention shifted to the force field. Just like her systems, it was pulsating erratically from the malfunction. Gia spent a long time trying to figure out how to get to the other side of the force field. She probed at the shimmering barrier, her sensors seeking any weakness, any fluctuation that might grant her passage. She tested various strategies to penetrate it and even more strategies to switch it off, but all attempts failed. Then, as if surrendering to its malfunctions, the force field flickered out of existence.

Gia sank to her knees beside Diego's lifeless body. She ran a quick check, even though she knew it would produce no satisfactory result. An influx of data that suddenly flooded her system cut her mourning short. Looking up, she realised the opaque dome that had obstructed the data stream was gone. Movement flickered at the edge of her sight. Gia's attention snagged, her systems choking on a surge of information. A figure had appeared in the drive-through, striding towards the facility. Gia ducked out of sight, taking refuge behind the scattered debris. Ms Mordwell casually navigated the carnage. The surrounding destruction held no intrigue, no hint of curiosity for her. Fallen Cybergang bodies, strewn about her path, meant nothing to her. She didn't spare them a glance, didn't flinch at the sight of their mangled corpses. With disinterested eyes, she stepped over them with her gaze fixed on the CerebroNet facility ahead.

As Ms Mordwell approached a large piece of debris from CerebroNet's wrecked facility blocking her path, she made a slight outward gesture with her palm. An energy tentacle sprang into action from her chest, crackling and snaking through the air with serpentine grace. The appendage lashed out, its gravitational force enveloping the slab of concrete. With a flick of her wrist, the energy limb hurled the debris aside as if it were as light as a feather. Once the path was clear, the limb retracted into the aperture on Ms Mordwell's chest. She continued towards the facility without even a flicker of concern on her face.

As Ms Mordwell stepped inside, she paused to scan the unfamiliar surroundings. Her eyes narrowed as she took in the location, her sensors probing the space for any signs of threat or opportunity. Soon, she oriented herself and, unobstructed, went deeper into the facility.

Gia followed close behind, her own sensors overclocked as she tracked Ms Mordwell's every step.

Ms Mordwell exuded a brisk determination. She emanated the aura of a woman no stranger to manipulation and control. Locks and hinges disintegrated under the controlled burn of her energy weapon, yet her face mirrored a placid lake—practised calm to conceal her anticipation.

Gia crept into the reactor room, trailing Ms Mordwell while maintaining a safe distance. She darted from one piece of equipment to another, using the machinery as cover to avoid detection. The room's exposed nature made stealth a challenge.

Ms Mordwell focused on cutting through the generator's thick walls. The metal hissed and billowed smoke under the intense heat of her energy weapon, providing an additional distraction. Gia seized the opportunity to crawl behind a stack of crates, hoping that the sound of the sizzling metal would mask any noise she might make. Peering around the edge of the crates, Gia watched as the last wall gave way. Ms Mordwell shoved the loose section to the ground, its metallic clatter echoing off the laboratory walls.

She paused, savouring the moment as she stood before the priceless pyrozetton. For the first time in her life, no barriers stood between her and the gateway to ultimate power. The pyrozetton's enigmatic surface shimmered, casting an ethereal glow across her face. Her fingers twitched with anticipation, eager to seize the power that lay just within her grasp. A smile tugged at her lips in a silent ecstasy of triumph. After a brief hesitation, she extended her hand, inching it towards the luminescent object. Reaching out with her index finger, she felt the gentle vibrations of its pulsing force. With bated breath and a reverent look, Ms Mordwell touched the pyrozetton.

Nothing happened.

Emboldened, she reached into the reactor, extracted the glowing object, and held it before her with triumphant glee. For a moment, she seemed entranced by the pyrozetton's continuous inversion and hypergeometric refraction of multi-dimensional crystalline recursions. Layer upon layer built upon itself, each facet reflecting a mirror of its own beginning. It was an ever-evolving entity. Ms Mordwell's eyes bored deep inside the pyrozetton, as if attempting to decode its secrets.

The hiss of an opening door sliced through the silence in the reactor room. Hiro stepped in, and his boots squeaked on the polished floor. He aimed his energy gun at Ms Mordwell. The weapon trembled in Hiro's hand—not from its weight, but from the intensity of his boiling emotions. He watched Ms Mordwell bask in the pulsating blue glow of the pyrozetton. The glare cast dramatic shadows that deepened the lines on her face and made her eyes glimmer with a malevolent intensity. It was a mixture of triumph, greed, and satisfaction from a decades-long ambition realised. Ms Mordwell's gaze remained fixed on the pyrozetton, drinking in its beauty and power as if she didn't notice Hiro. Only a flicker of annoyance crossed her face. The slight tightening at the corners of her eyes and a brief purse of her lips gave away her irritation at the interruption of her triumph.

Ms Mordwell let out a sigh and turned to face Hiro. Her voice dripped with affection as she said, 'Look who has finally decided to join us. For a while, I thought I'd lost you. It's so good to see you again.'

Hiro's eyes narrowed, burning with hatred. 'The feeling isn't mutual. Your face is never a welcome sight.'

Ms Mordwell chuckled, unfazed by his hostility. 'Please, Hiro, don't be bitter. It doesn't suit a man with your potential. You hold more power than you know and need to start behaving like it.'

'I do know. The pyrozetton you are holding connects me with another universe.'

'It sounds like you found your mummy in the end.'

'I also know you killed everyone who loved me.'

'I didn't kill your mummy or your friends. You did.'

'You made me!' Hiro roared, his voice echoing through the room. Realising his mistake, he took a deep breath. He didn't want to give her the pleasure of seeing him suffer. Pulling himself together required immense effort.

'You're just like me, Hiro. You put on a tough exterior, but deep down, you know we're fighting for the same thing. I couldn't have done this without you,' Ms Mordwell replied, sounding serene. She rotated the pyrozetton, watching the light refract off it. 'Most people don't understand that progress requires bold action. But you do. Paying Fassal for you was the best investment I ever made.'

Hiro's heart pounded, and his grip on the energy gun tightened. 'Did you brainwash the old man, too?' he asked, struggling to keep his voice steady.

Mordwell shook her head, her smile unwavering as she took a few steps closer to Hiro. 'I didn't lay a finger on the man. When I heard about a guy who could hunt the Eyeballs, I knew it could only be you. Fassal didn't even hesitate to accept my offer. When I visited your community, I could feel your presence. It was one of the happiest moments of my life. I knew then the search was over.' She took another step closer. 'Open your mind to the truth. The only way forward for humanity is to evolve beyond our current limitations. I need you, and deep down, you know you need me too.'

'What I need is for you to give me the pyrozetton.'

'You'll have it soon enough. Join me. We must work together for a better future. For humanity's progress. Just imagine the world we can create together, free from the suffering and limitations that plague humanity.'

'Is destruction your idea of progress? You destroy everything in your path. You dissected people for parts, bombed government buildings, and killed CerebroNet.' Hiro gestured with the energy gun at the pyrozetton. 'All that just to get this shiny thing.'

'You misunderstand me, Hiro. All those sacrifices were necessary. I'm not destroying anything. I'm clearing the way for something better to emerge. Just like a wildfire clears the dead brush for fresh growth. Sometimes, creation demands sacrifice.' Mordwell locked eyes with his. 'As I said before, you and I are more alike than you want to admit. You so desperately wanted to destroy CerebroNet. I gave you what you wanted. Even more, I let you do it. I let you experience it, and you loved it. I felt your satisfaction when you fired the first missile. So don't lecture me about destruction.'

A grimace twisted Hiro's face, revealing the depth of his mental anguish as her words hit home. Hiro squinted, and his brows knitted together, but he said nothing.

Encouraged by his silence, Mordwell continued. 'Join me, Hiro,' she urged again. 'Together, we can shape our useless species, plagued by self-destruction, into a new civilisation. A civilisation evolved into a single mind driven by ambition and greatness.' Her voice dropped low, filled with a chilling certainty. 'Look, Hiro. Your mom abandoned you. Mr Fassal sold you out. I know it hurts, but please don't allow this suffering to be for nothing. Let me show you how to channel this pain and turn it into humanity's success.'

Hiro felt the sting of betrayal all over again, and a part of him flared up in rage. Recognising this was what Ms Mordwell wanted, he suppressed the emotion. 'I don't think everyone has to pay for my mistakes. Unlike you, I don't want to destroy humanity. I want to protect it.'

'What humanity? The one that sliced the world in two so the privileged few can feast on the misery and suffering of the masses? What's humane about it? Perhaps the humanity that raced for greater profits until it consumed the entire ecosystem? Are we speaking of the same humanity? The one hard-wired for mutual destruction? Humanity had the opportunity to change for the better countless times, but we have chosen not to again and again. Take a hard look. We thrive on hatred and jealousy. You need to wake up to the truth that we're addicted to annihilation. We are still armed to the teeth with nuclear weapons. We are stupid. We destroyed our only habitable planet. Open your eyes! Humanity slaughtered itself a long time ago. Now it's decomposing. I am offering change, an evolution, or we go extinct.'

Hiro just blinked at Mordwell's cynical worldview. Even with his little knowledge of history, the past painted a brutal picture, but he couldn't shake off the feeling Ms Mordwell was setting a trap for him again. 'You omit everything good about humanity,' Hiro argued. 'There is empathy, kindness, art—'

'Art is just a byproduct of a bored mind. Try stopping floods and droughts with your art. What has your art done for the starving children? People are wasting their brain power on things like art. All these useless desires—the need to be someone, the necessity to be seen and to matter. What is all this worth if all die?' Ms Mordwell's eyes sparkled predatorily, almost gleefully. 'But humanity still has a last chance. We can become that last opportunity. We can link humanity's mental capacity into a single, collective entity, ensuring that the sacrifices of generations before us are not in vain. Our new collective intelligence will have a shared mission—to flourish.'

Ms Mordwell paused, reading Hiro's face. When she continued, her voice escalated in intensity. 'Just imagine what we could achieve, Hiro. With your DNA and the pyrozetton, we will override individual weakness and helplessness. We will eradicate their suffering. We will be a single consciousness where each brain functions as a cell of one powerful mind. Just imagine a world where all people are finally united and have a common goal.'

Hiro was stunned with disbelief. 'You are insane! Do you even hear yourself? You see humanity as some simple organism, a virus competing for resources. You purposefully dismiss everything good—empathy, love.'

'Love is an ingenious tool of nature that compels human animals to breed and produce offspring. Love is just hormones—a drug, and when the high is gone, we end up with little copies of ourselves, so we can consume more, gain a competitive advantage, and have more power.'

'You know nothing about love. I loved my friend Diego, and he loved me. We built a world full of laughter, understanding, and support. We didn't need to rule the world to be happy. Our world, filled with empathy and love, was enough. But you destroyed it all. I loved Gia, our new friend. But you killed her, too. Gia, a robot, was more human than you ever will be. You made me kill everyone who loved me because you're unable to feel love yourself, and nobody truly ever loved you back. Look at what you've become—pure evil.'

Ms Mordwell laughed aloud. 'You are so naive. You don't get it, do you? Let me try one more time. Your mum's crystalline generator heated plasmas to temperatures much hotter than the sun's core. When that reactor overloaded, it didn't create the pyrozetton. It opened a door through the fabric of the universe. The pyrozetton is that door. Someone will come through it from the other side. Do you understand? These beings are able to give DNA to non-organic objects. Just think how powerful these creatures are.' Ms Mordwell fixed her gaze on the pyrozetton in her hand. 'When they come through, they will not be concerned with your petty art and stupid love, just as we aren't concerned about the daily quarrels of rats. Even if we succeed in reversing the climate catastrophe, they will come through one day. We need to be ready to face them. Forget your friends and family. If we don't evolve, we all will perish.'

Hiro's jaw clenched, his teeth grinding together as he stared at Ms Mordwell. 'No, we won't. Only you,' he retorted in a low, trembling voice. He pressed the trigger, feeling the whir of the plasma blaster as it fired. The energy blast erupted from the barrel, slamming into her with a blinding flash of light.

But Hiro's assault washed over Ms Mordwell's personal force field like water against an impenetrable dam. The translucent barrier rippled and shimmered with iridescent light as the charge dissipated into nothingness, like raindrops evaporating on scorching metal.

Hiro blinked rapidly as bewilderment washed over his face, his mind struggling to accept the foreboding consequences of his failure. His thumb jumped to push the setting dial, but already cranked to its limit, it wouldn't budge. An icy terror replaced his confusion as he verified the setting. His eyes widened in dismay, and a bead of cold sweat trickled down his temple.

Ms Mordwell's sniggering was a cold, grating rasp that sent shivers racing down Hiro's spine like nails scratching a chalkboard. Her eyes blazed with bitter disappointment, and the lines of her face hardened into a mask of contempt. 'I don't have the patience for this,' she declared, her voice dripping with disdain, each word sharp as a razor. 'You will help me whether you want to or not.'

In an instant, Hiro felt a constricting force around his neck, as if an invisible noose had tightened around his throat. Ms Mordwell's energy limb, a lasso-like extension of her will, coiled around him, strangling him with unrelenting force. He clawed at the tendril, his fingers scrabbling against the shimmering tentacle as he desperately fought to free himself, his lungs burning for air. But his struggles only intensified the constriction. The pressure increased until dark spots began dancing before his eyes, and his vision blurred at the edges. The room faded into darkness as oxygen deprivation took hold. His mind raced, consumed by a primal survival instinct. In a surge of desperation, Hiro thrust a trembling hand into his pocket and pulled out the portable EMP device he had taken from Gia's den—the same device he had once considered using to end his own life. Now, it was his last hope of saving it. With a last burst of strength, he smashed the EMP against the shimmering tendril and jabbed his finger on the red button.

The tentacle absorbed the electromagnetic pulse, and the crackling surge of energy rushed along its length towards Mordwell's personal force field. Her shield collapsed in a dazzling explosion, the shockwave flinging the pyrozetton from her grasp and hurling her and Hiro against the opposite walls like rag dolls. The room filled with the acrid smell of burning electronics.

The massive energy discharge awakened the pyrozetton. The object spun lazily in mid-air as it flushed radiant rays of light across the room, painting the walls with a kaleidoscope of colours. It emanated a soft hum. The sound reverberated in Hiro's bones, calling to him like a siren's song. He crawled towards it, the metallic scent of ozone filling his nostrils and light blurred into a dizzying array of colours. The room seemed to warp around him, expanding and contracting like a breathing organism. He reached for the pyrozetton, his fingers mere inches away, but his augmented body, battered and drained, betrayed him. With a final, desperate lunge, Hiro collapsed back to the floor.

Disoriented, Ms Mordwell staggered to her feet, her head

pounding. She cast a sweeping glance around the room. Her eyes narrowed as they locked onto the spinning pyrozetton. Beside her, Hiro's weapon, marred by scorch marks, emitted occasional sparks from its damaged core. Ms Mordwell snatched up the gun, her fingers curling around the grip as she approached Hiro. Her eyes flashed with barely contained rage. 'Troublemaker,' she sneered, levelling the weapon at him, her finger tightening on the trigger.

Hiro met Ms Mordwell's gaze, his heart racing in his chest, pounding against his ribs like a caged animal. But just as Mordwell's finger began to squeeze the trigger, Gia burst out from her hiding place, a jagged piece of debris clutched in her hand. With a swift, fluid motion, she plunged the sharp edge into Ms Mordwell's neck. The impact sent a shudder through her body. Ms Mordwell bellowed in pain, her face contorting in rage as she lurched forward, swinging around to aim the energy weapon at Gia. The blast caught the robot in the chest, sending her sprawling across the lab in a shower of sparks and twisted alloys.

Seeing Gia alive, Hiro felt a surge of joy so intense it nearly overwhelmed him, a sob escaping his lips in a release of the despair he didn't know he was holding back. But the joy was short-lived as a fresh wave of dread crashed over him, watching Gia suffer again because of him, her body jerking and twitching on the floor.

Gia struggled to her feet, her movements jerky and uncoordinated, sparks flying from her damaged circuits. Ms Mordwell advanced on her with fury etched into every line of her face. Her energy whip wrapped around Gia's neck. She began slamming the robot against the ceiling and the floor, the brutal impacts cracking the surfaces with each blow as she, again and again, jerked Gia's body up and down. Finally, Ms Mordwell paused, holding Gia's body dangling on her energy lasso. She savoured the inflicted damage with a satisfied expression on her face. 'You're difficult to kill,' she said, amused by Gia's involuntary twitches.

Hiro's yell cut through the chaos from behind Ms Mordwell, his voice raw with desperation. 'Let her go, or I'll fry your precious pyrozetton!'

Ms Mordwell's eyes narrowed to pinpricks, her breath hissing out through clenched teeth. With deliberate slowness, she turned to face Hiro, Gia still hanging from her tentacle like a broken doll.

Hiro stood with his arm outstretched, holding the portable EMP device a hair's breadth away from the pyrozetton. His thumb hovered over the red button as he trembled with barely contained rage. 'Leave her alone, bitch. You and I can continue this conversation another day. Otherwise, say goodbye to the pyrozetton and your dreams of world dominance.'

To Hiro's shock, Ms Mordwell threw her head back and burst out laughing, the sound echoing through the lab—a hyena-like cackle that sent icy shivers racing down his spine. Goosebumps prickled across his skin as his mind grappled with Mordwell's unexpected reaction, trying to understand what she was playing at.

Gia tumbled to the floor as Ms Mordwell released her grip. In a blur of motion, the energy limb whipped towards Hiro and snatched the EMP device from his hand, leaving him grasping at empty air.

'You stupid, stupid boy,' Mordwell cackled. A triumphant grin spread across her face as she watched the panic creep into Hiro's eyes.

As Hiro recovered from the initial shock, he stretched out his hand to grab the pyrozetton, his fingers closing around its shifting surface. But as he touched it, his head snapped back, and his mouth fell open in a silent scream. Blinding light erupted from his eyes and mouth, three searing rays that converged on the ceiling above him. The beams swirled together, forming a whirlpool of energy that solidified and exploded, raining down a million glittering crystals.

For a heartbeat, the crystals hung suspended in the air, like stars frozen in time, in a breathtaking display of shimmering beauty. Then, with a high-pitched whoop, they darted towards each other, coalescing into a massive octagonal portal that yawned open above Hiro's head. The portal's inky void swallowed the rays of light, drawing them into its swirling abyss of darkness.

The lab erupted into chaos as the portal's pull intensified, sucking in everything not bolted down. Lab tools and debris pelted Gia and Ms Mordwell as the void drew them towards itself. The larger pieces of equipment and furniture followed, slamming into them with bone-jarring force.

The pull of the portal became difficult to fight as the invisible force tugged at their bodies with increasing strength. Gia dug her robotic fingers into a piece of equipment anchored to the floor, clinging to it with all her strength as the portal's suction threatened to tear her away.

As loose items vanished into the void, panic flashed across Ms Mordwell's face as she grasped the danger she was in. Her eyes darted around the lab, looking for a way to fight against the inexorable pull. But before she could find a way out of the perilous situation, her feet left the ground, and she began floating towards the portal, her limbs flailing in the air. In a desperate, split-second decision, she lashed out her energy tentacle, tethering herself to Gia in a last-ditch attempt at salvation. Suspended in the air, they trembled like leaves in a gale wind as the portal's pull grew even stronger.

The void didn't affect Hiro. He stood utterly still, seemingly oblivious to the chaos raging around him, with the pyrozetton clutched tightly in his hand.

Ms Mordwell saw the opportunity. She stretched her arm, trying to grab the pyrozetton from Hiro, but she kept missing it as the violent juddering kept it from her grasp.

Gia screamed as the combined force of their mass strained against her grip, threatening to rip her fingers from their sockets. Ms Mordwell's gaze darted to Gia, and she realised that if Gia's fingers failed, they would both be swallowed by the endless darkness. With a growl of frustration, she released her hold on

Gia. Her energy limb latched onto the pyrozetton.

For a breathless moment, they seemed locked in a tense standoff—Hiro holding the pyrozetton, Ms Mordwell tethered to it, and her frightened gaze fixed on it in anticipation. She felt her fate hang in the balance as she dangled on her energy lasso, mere meters from the portal's hungry void.

The gamble played out in her favour. Neither the pyrozetton nor Hiro yielded, the device remaining firmly in his grasp. Triumph flashed across Ms Mordwell's face. Using her energy limb as a lifeline, she inched closer to the pyrozetton with each desperate hand-over-hand movement, straining against the portal's pull. Muscles burning, heart pounding, Ms Mordwell gritted her teeth and pressed on, refusing to surrender to the portal's insatiable appetite, determined to claim her prize.

Gia's eyes hardened as she watched Ms Mordwell's escape attempt. Fury boiled up inside her like a volcano, ready to erupt. 'Don't even think about it, bitch!' she yelled as she released her grip on the equipment, surrendering herself to the portal's embrace.

Gia slammed into Ms Mordwell with the force of a battering ram. The impact dislodged the pyrozetton from Hiro's grasp. Gia and Ms Mordwell tumbled across the threshold of the portal in an uncontrolled spin. As the pyrozetton, clutched by the energy limb, disappeared into the void, the crystal octagon portal collapsed in on itself, crumpling out of existence.

Hiro fell onto the floor. Silence descended upon the lab, broken only by the ragged sound of his breathing.

* * *

Hiro opened his eyes. The weight of his failure immediately crushed him like a physical blow. He felt hollow, as if his essence had been drained away, leaving behind nothing but an empty shell. With a herculean effort, he forced himself to his feet. Staggering through CerebroNet's facility, he wandered aimlessly, adrift in a sea of hopelessness. He felt exhausted and overwhelmed by a profound sense of loss. Nothing mattered anymore. The corridors felt alien and hostile.

He found himself back at the entrance, next to Diego's lifeless body. A fresh wave of grief crashed over him, and he fell to his knees beside his dead friend. With trembling hands, he cradled Diego's head in his lap, his fingers gently brushing his cold skin. A wail of anguish tore from Hiro's throat echoing through the empty halls. Diego's lifeless eyes stared back at him, a haunting reminder that he would never again see the friendly smile or hear that contagious laughter. Tears streamed down Hiro's face, falling onto Diego's still features. 'Forgive me,' he whispered over and over again, knowing his plea would never receive an answer.

A sizzling sound and the acrid smell of ozone jolted Hiro from his mourning. A cascade of glowing sparks exploded before his eyes, swirling and dancing in the air like fireflies. The sparks coalesced into a radiant spiral of light, buzzing with intense energy. The spiral expanded, its edges shimmering with pearlescent blues and shimmering golds, painting the room in an ethereal glow. The light pulsed faster and faster until it burst forth in a shower of glittering sparks that crystallised into a massive octagonal portal. Iridescent light filled the portal's frame, refracting off its crystalline structure in a dazzling display of colour.

Hiro squinted against the blinding light, confused by the sudden display of ethereal beauty. A figure materialised within the shimmering aura, growing larger with each step as it approached from the other side. As the figure drew closer, Hiro's eyes widened in disbelief. The outline, the gait, the piercing stare—it couldn't be. But there, stepping out of the portal with a smile on his handsome face, was Diego.

Hiro's gaze darted back and forth between the lifeless body in his lap and the impossible apparition before him. His mouth opened and closed, but no words came out, only a strangled gasp of shock.

The new Diego surveyed the scene, his expression mixed with amusement and sorrow. 'At least I know I'll look pretty when I die,' he quipped, his voice achingly familiar. Then, his face grew serious, and he stretched out his hand towards Hiro in invitation. 'You have nothing left in this world,' he said softly as his piercing eyes burrowed deep into Hiro with genuine intensity. 'Come with me. You can't help him anymore, but you can help me. And you can help Gia. You owe her.' He wiggled his fingers, beckoning Hiro forward. 'Come. She needs you.'

Hiro sensed the pyrozetton's vibrations seeping through the portal and, for a moment, the taste of defeat was so bitter it made him gag. He stared into the bright light of the portal. His mind reeled with the memories of all he had endured. He choked on the bitter disappointment at the memory of his community's betrayal. He remembered his mother's plea to keep the pyrozetton away from Ms Mordwell. Yet, the architect of his misery had escaped with it, leaving him with the memories of his ultimate failure. He remembered despising CerebroNet—only to learn it was his mother—who was destroyed because of his naivety. Hiro thought of his brutally murdered father. He felt regret at becoming a tool for Ms Mordwell's sadistic machinations, forcing him to shoot Gia. He cried out loud at the memory of Diego's forgiving eyes as he strangled him against the electrocuting force field. There was truly nothing good left for him in this world but pain and regret.

His hands shaking, Hiro brushed away the tears that streaked his face. Gently, he laid Diego's head on the cold floor, his fingers lingering for a moment in a silent farewell. Then he stood up, squared his shoulders and faced the portal and the impossible figure that looked at him with inviting eyes. He reached out, clasped the hand of Diego's double, and stepped with him into the glittering octagon.

Thank you for joining Hiro's journey in *The Birth of Cogenant*. The story continues in **Book 2**: ***The Penance of Cogenant***.

Get Your FREE Prequel Story

See what happened right before Chapter 1!

As a special thank you for reading, get your **FREE** exclusive short story, ***Droid Hunter's Folly***. Discover the crucial events that set Hiro's journey in motion.

You'll also be the first to know when The Penance of Cogenant launches, plus updates on Book 3.

Subscribe to receive your free story in your inbox:

www.cogenant.com/subscribe

Help Other Readers Discover Cogenant

Your support means everything. If you enjoyed this book, please consider leaving a star rating or review—it's the best way to help new readers find Hiro's story.

Leave a rating or review on Amazon, Goodreads, Kobo, or wherever you bought this book.